THE WARSAW GAMBIT

Benjamin Lloyd

Copyright © 2023 Benjamin Lloyd

All rights reserved.

ISBN: 9798873321780

The scenarios in this book are fictitious. Any similarity to actual persons, living or dead, is coincidental.

For Linda, the love of my life.
Your encouragement and belief made this happen.

Chapter One

Jankowski was shaking. He felt like he had just seen a ghost. He looked at his hastily scribbled notes and realised he may not have seen one, but he had definitely *heard* from one.

And now it was his turn to come back from the dead.

***

Despite the automatic glance to his left, Warner almost missed the signal, two yellow chalk stripes on the side of Church of the Holiest Saviour on Zbawiciela Place. Hardly surprising though, the Cold War had ended nearly thirty-five years ago, all of his contacts long since retired. Enjoying the luxuries of imperialist capitalism no doubt. Unless they had died of course. He only came this way from a 30-something year old habit, a slight detour on his way to buy a newspaper and milk from the Żabka grocery store down the block from his apartment. The same steps, the same sideways glance, the same sense of disappointment when there was nothing to see. And yet today…

He took another look, convinced the stripes must be some kind of coincidence, just local kids messing around. But there they were, fresh, two bold yellow lines clearly visible on the crumbling grey concrete. It had to be a joke because the man behind the chalk was dead, had been for decades.

Having nothing better to do, he brushed the chalk off with his sleeve and walked on towards Park Belwederski and the long-dead dead drop his long-dead contact had used to pass SB secrets. *For old times sake*, he muttered grinning to himself as he walked through the wrought iron gates. At least it would give someone a laugh, even if it was at his expense. Maybe he was about to be the star of a new CIA hidden camera show.

It was already mid-morning but the sun was weak and a light mist hovered above the carefully manicured lawns. Joggers and dog walkers weaved their way through the trees, appearing and disappearing in the damp fog and shadows, casting long shadows across the dew fringed leaves.

Warner made his own meandering trek through the park, darting behind hedges and doubling back to check if he was being followed. *Old habits*, he smiled, approaching a low retaining wall behind an empty flowerbed. He was wheezing with exertion, and his forehead was damp with sweat under the battered brown homburg he wore. His waistline expansion was inversely proportional to his level of fitness, so Warner took the opportunity to catch his breath and carry out a final check for watchers. Satisfied he wasn't being observed, he pulled a damp, mossy brick from the wall and felt in the space behind. He didn't honestly expect to find anything, but who doesn't like to collect assorted filth under their fingernails?

He jumped as his fingers brushed against something

in the hole then, pulse quickening, forced himself to grab hold of the mystery object. But it wasn't a mystery, it was a small metal tube. He unscrewed it to extract a small, rolled-up piece of very thin tissue paper - but he already knew what it said.

A broad smile spread across his chubby face. *Just like the good old days.* But how?

***

His brain was still sharp, but he was completely out of practice so it had taken him some time to remember the correct rules of a meet. Originally he had planned to arrive fifteen minutes early to check the location for surveillance but then he remembered that there wouldn't be any. It was hardly likely that Jankowski would be under observation - the man was long dead. The SB had been disbanded in 1989 when democracy had finally arrived in Poland, so there were no secret police to worry about either. No one would care about an old Cold War warrior like him either - assuming they even recognised him. This had to be an elaborate joke by another bored old man like himself. Maybe one of the old crowd from Warsaw Station playing a trick.

At 4pm he opened the door to the bar and immediately spotted Jankowski sat at a table in the shadows at the back of the room. Clichéed? Perhaps. But that's because it works.

The long room was quite full, students piling in from the nearby Politechnika Warszawska as lectures finished for the day. All of the tables and chairs were occupied and there was a crush of thirsty undergraduates waiting at the bar. The grey heads of Warner and Jankowski would have been quite conspicuous if the SB had still been on the look out for capitalist spies. But now they could pass for ageing academics out for an extracurricular drink.

Jankowski stood as Warner approached his table. He was the epitome of average - average height, average grey hair, average looks, average clothes. Indeed, his complete lack of remarkableness is exactly why he had been so successful in his work for the SB - and his CIA handlers. The only thing that wasn't average was his sharp, unblinking eyes that missed nothing. He had barely changed at all since they had last met.

"The waiter recommends the pierogi," Jankowski opened, his face betraying no emotion at all.

"Today I have a taste for gołąbki," countered Warner.

They stared at each other for a moment, then burst into laughter. Jankowski grabbed Warner and embraced him, slapping him on the back, before nudging his towards the bench on the opposite side of the table. "Your accent is still terrible. But I have missed you my old friend. How have you been? I thought you had returned to America?"

"I did, for a few years. But it seems I went native, your miserable city is in my blood. I've been living here for a quarter of a century now."

"And you never thought to visit me for vodka?" Jankowski asked, pretending to be offended.

"Probably because you are dead. I read the reports myself."

"Even though most Poles just wanted to forget everything that happened, some wanted 'justice'. So they started hunting down former SB agents. 'Dying' seemed like a good way not to *die*."

"Thank God."

"Thank God indeed."

"So, what brings me here today? You just wanted to see if the CIA was still active in Warsaw? Maybe find someone to talk with about the old days?"

"*Nie*, I have important news. *Really* important intel," Jankowski was completely deadpan.

I doubt it, Warner thought, stroking his chin in the universal sign of disbelief. "You can't have known that I would see the dead drop signal? Or that I would act - you're dead after all."

"*Nie*, I just hoped that someone from Warsaw Station would recognise the old ways. I needed to get someone's attention - and I did not know you were still here."

"Important intel? Why not stop by the embassy? You know you're allowed to just walk in there these days, right?"

"I tried. I went to Ujazdowskie and asked to speak to a field agent, but they refused. No one would listen. No one cares. They didn't believe me."

"OK," sighed Warner, "So what is it? What didn't they believe?"

"I know how to end the war in Ukraine before it spreads or turns nuclear. Because I know *exactly* where Leontin will be on April 27th. Maybe they will listen to you."

***

Warner had nearly laughed in the old man's face. But the longer they talked, the clearer it became that Jankowski was telling the truth. His intel had always been good, completely accurate and even thirty something years later he was still on the ball.

According to Jankowski's source, Leontin had an important meeting scheduled at the President's official dacha at Dolgiye Borody, a small village about half-way between Moscow and Saint Petersburg. Built for Stalin, although it is said that he hated the silence of the countryside so much he only visited once. It took five years to build, using the same design as his dacha at Volyn but he…"

"We can talk about Stalin's hatred of spruce forests another time," Warner interrupted, steering Jankowski back on topic, "Tell me about this meeting."

"My source does not know why, but Leontin believes the meeting is so important and so sensitive that it must be held in person in a place he feels safe. The date cannot be changed so Leontin *has* to be there."

"Who is he meeting?" Warner pushed, "Who holds that much power over him?"

"I don't know because my source did not say. Maybe my source does not know yet. But it's big. Important. Top secret and essential. That is what my source is telling me, *essential*"

"And who is your source?"

"You still ask the same questions after all these years! But this time if I tell you it was the elderly housekeeper at the dacha you would not believe me."

"Is it the elderly housekeeper at Dolgiye Borody?"

"Yes, of course!"

Jankowski was right, Warner did not believe him.

He had never figured out where the old SB man got his information. His sources were always anonymous and their contact infrequent - but they were never wrong. Warner had built his own career on them, so they had to be highly placed - and trusted - in the Russian government.

Working with Langley, Warsaw Station had tried, and failed, to identify any of Jankowski's sources in the hope of establishing direct contact. But Jankowski had always been a smart player, each drop containing nothing more than the most important details to protect his sources - and to keep himself in the loop.

So despite his impeccable track record, it was now up to Warner to convince the CIA to take Jankowski's bombshell seriously. *Fat chance*, he thought, *they're just going to laugh their asses off.*

"As much as I enjoyed the dead drop, I guess it's redundant now," said Warner, "Why don't we just agree to meet back here at the same time tomorrow? Then I can tell you what the Agency have decided to do."

"*Nie*, we will meet at my apartment and drink vodka. I hope they kill the bastard."

They shook hands, grinning like kids. They were back in the game.

***

Back in his own apartment, Warner looked at the clock. It would be 11am in Langley so he could pass on the message without getting anyone out of bed. Even if it turned out to be the useless ramblings of an old man who missed the thrills of the past, at least he wasn't going to piss anyone off. He dialled through to the Europe desk in the ugly, squat building back Stateside.

The young analyst who took the call had no idea who Warner was. He could hear her tap-tapping his access codes into her computer followed by a sigh of exasperation when his name and credentials were verified. He could imagine the young woman rolling her eyes in frustration at a colleague on the desk opposite. Switching to an encrypted line, Warner was invited to share his intel. The analyst scribbled the details onto her notepad before promising to pass the info to Russia desk team for actioning. Her second promise of a return call was even less convincing.

Chapter Two

Warner was roused by a persistent knocking on his door. He had been by the phone all night waiting for Langley to call back, eventually falling asleep in his threadbare armchair as the first shafts of dawn sunlight peeked around the edges of the faded and tatty curtains.

He rubbed the sleep from his bleary eyes and stumbled to the door of his apartment. He was surprised to find a well-dressed young American man waiting impatiently.

"Can I come in and have a word? I'm here from Warsaw Station," he said, sharp and business-like.

Warner gestured towards the small sitting room on the left, encouraging the young man to take a seat on the sofa, "Tea?"

The analyst looked in disgust at the aged furniture and shook his head. He had been told to stroke the old man's ego, to make him feel valued. Quite the star when he was an agent thanks to a source who seemed to have a direct line to the Kremlin. He had glanced at Warner's file and career track record before making the visit, but the truth was he didn't care for these old Cold War warriors and their insane conspiracy theories. He looked again at the cluttered bookshelves, dusty sills and dog-eared beige wallpaper. The old bastard had let himself go, maybe he'd actually gone native.

He shook his head again. "No, thank you. Listen, I won't take up too much of your time Mr Warner," he began, "I just wanted to let you know that the Agency is appreciative of your efforts yesterday and we will take it from here. Although the Russia desk at Langley was more than a little annoyed at the way you breached protocol."

He was oily and unconvincing, greasy as his slicked-back hair and unable to contain a condescending tone voice as he relayed their displeasure.

"Naturally." The young man's disinterest and disrespect irritated Warner and he knew he was about to be dismissed by this jumped-up little prick in his designer suit and handmade Italian leather shoes.

"Naturally. We don't really expect much from this one, the Cold War has been over for decades after all. But we'll pass it up the chain, so to speak." The man just wanted to leave, to get out of the filthy time warp he was standing in.

"Naturally," said Warner again. "And if Jankowski tries to make contact again?"

"We'll take a look at what he's given us first. If it's any good, then one my team will take over running the asset. Personally I doubt there will be anything to do."

"Naturally."

"Anyway, thanks again for your help," the young, nameless man said. "I'll see myself out."

He started walking towards the door and then paused, "Oh, one other thing Mr Warner. Langley was very clear. I must warn you, whatever happens, you are to leave it to the the serving officers."

"Naturally."

And just like that, the annoying young man was gone.

***

Two men huddled around a desk in a small, poorly-lit office in the Kremlin.

"It seems that Jankowski has reactivated himself in Warsaw," the younger of the men said, passing a short printout to the blue-suited man on his left.

"Should we be worried?" Alexey Sokolov was the head of the Presidential Security Service, SPB for short. A small sub-directorate dedicated to a single task - protecting the Russian president. Which is probably why he looked like a bouncer, short brown hair, broad shoulders and a nose that looked like it had been battered a few times.

"He was a serious problem in the 80s and 90s. A devious bastard too, always had accurate intel sourced from the highest levels of the KGB and other government agencies," the younger man continued, "We'd never have identified him if the Americans hadn't been so lazy after Perestroika."

"Why did we not deal with him then?"

"Because apparently *we* were lazy bastards too. That and the fact he died before we got to him anyway"

"So he's reactivated *and* back from the dead. Do we know what was said? Or where his new information came from?"

"No, we have no idea. But he must have felt it was important - or valuable."

Sokolov drew hard on his cigarette and stared at the

ceiling. The President had something big planned and the SPB had been placed on high alert, but what damage could an old Cold War warrior really do? After a moment he turned back to his subordinate, "If Jankowski wants to play by the old rules, then he can suffer the old consequences."

The younger man nodded and hurried from the room.

Chapter Three

Warner was making his regular morning walk back from Żabka scanning headlines in the paper; the WiS government arguing for increased tariffs on Ukrainian wheat, more refugees streaming across the Polish border, disputes with EU, riots in France and the Netherlands, work beginning to repair the Nord Stream gas pipeline after it had been blown up by persons unknown, accusations of Russian and EU interference in the upcoming election. A steady flow of bad news.

    He looked up as he passed the Church, noting the three yellow stripes chalked on the wall. He could feel his pulse pounding as he recognised Jankowski's distress signal indicating that something serious had happened since yesterday. Rather than go directly to the emergency dead letterbox, he broke with protocol and headed north for Jankowski's apartment in the Śródmieście district instead. As soon as he turned into the street he could see something was wrong. A small crowd was being held back by uniformed police outside the building who watched as a covered gurney was loaded into the back of a fluorescent orange ambulance.

    He joined the back of the small, jostling throng, listening to the chatter.

"An old man, fell down the stairs," a motherly looking woman was saying to her neighbour.

"Down the stairs? I heard he fell over the balcony," said the other woman, arms crossed with a cigarette hanging from the corner of her mouth.

"Well yes, he fell over the balcony on the stairs," sniffed the mother.

"Must have been drinking then. It's not easy to fall over a railing like that. Although I do remember…"

Warner drifted away from the crowd. Something was very, very wrong. Jankowski was in good health and, like the woman had said, people don't just fall over railings. *He also had time to leave the emergency signal*, Warner thought, *he already knew something was off*. More importantly, it meant that Jankowski had left something in the backup dead drop.

He turned the corner and waited for a moment staring into a shop window. In the reflection he saw a little man in a flat worker's cap come around the corner on the other side of the road, stopping when he caught sight of Warner. He had one of those instantly forgettable faces that would allow him to blend into any crowd, so unremarkable that no one would ever notice him - unless they had been trained to spot field agents. Warner moved off again, noting that the man continued to follow, never quite catching up or over-taking.

He was definitely being followed by a professional although he couldn't tell whether the tail was American, Russian, Polish or something else entirely. If the FSB knew Jankowski's secret, they would want to tie up any loose ends - including Warner. Or maybe the CIA had him followed to ensure he kept his promise and stayed out of official business. He could confront the man and ask, but the killing of Jankowski suggested that would be a risky, potentially fatal, move. The good news was that whoever he represented, the man in the hat was alone, which meant that the former CIA man had a far better chance of losing him.

Warner's tradecraft took over. He switched his cellphone off and dropped it casually into a nearby trash can as he passed. Then turned towards the busier streets, joining a steady stream of people on Marszałkowska Street heading north into the city centre. He tried to blend in with the crowd for a few blocks before darting left into the Hotel Metropol. He walked briskly through the lobby nodding politely to the receptionist sat behind her desk, before taking a door on the left into the hotel carpark and circling back to the front of the hotel.

Confident that he had been seen and followed into the hotel, Warner ran down a set of stairs into a large underpass below the road. Thankfully there were still plenty of people down here, browsing a small arcade of shops or crossing into the old town. He thrust a 20 złoty note into the hands of one of the stallholders and grabbed a baseball cap which he screwed down hard on his head. Slowing pace slightly, he merged with the crowd once more, taking another flight of stairs upwards, back into the light at street level.

Opposite the Hotel Metropol, he started to head south, back the way he had come. Warner could see the man in the hat standing just outside the hotel, scanning the crowds. Clearly he had lost his target. *Still got it*, Warner grinned to himself.

After a block, he re-crossed Marszałkowska Street and into the shadows of Żurawia. Up ahead he could see trees, marking the park surrounding St Barbara's church - and the backup dead letter drop. He took a seat on a bench by the churchyard gate that allowed him to watch people coming and going, hurrying through the park on their way back to work after lunch. Warner was grateful of the opportunity to catch his breath - it had been nearly thirty years since he last had to shake a tail. For the first time he realised that maybe he really was too old for this game.

After waiting and watching for five minutes he was sure that no one was following. He moved carefully through the gravestones until he found the one he was looking for. Marta Mackiewicz's grave was slightly raised, with a narrow gap just under the lip of the heavy stone covering where the mortar had crumbled and fallen away. Warner took one last look to make sure he wasn't being observed, then stuck his index finger into the hole to retrieve an envelope which went straight into his jacket pocket.

As he left the churchyard, Warner realised he couldn't go home. Whoever was watching Jankowski knew about him too - and they would probably be watching his apartment. He wandered aimlessly for a few blocks with the sudden realisation that Jankowski really was dead this time - and that whoever killed him was probably *very* interested in him too. Eventually he found himself outside a milk bar back on Marszałkowska, so he grabbed himself a bowl of bright red borscht and some slices of bread, taking them to a battered formica-topped table in the corner.

After a few spoonfuls of the thin beetroot broth, he retrieved the envelope from his pocket and tore it open. Inside there were several pages of Jankowski's spidery handwriting. Most were a recap of what they had discussed yesterday - where to find Leontin and how he had come by the information. But there was also a cover letter addressed to Warner directly.

***

Warner,

So here we are my friend - I survived the Cold War and escaped the clutches of the SB. How ironic that I should finally be caught by by the FSB with the assistance of my old friends, the CIA!

It seems that Mr Leontin may have friends in strange places, and now they are coming for me. Unfortunately, that means that you are probably in danger too.

I don't know what you want to do with this information, but hopefully you can find someone who will listen - and act.

Do powodzenia my friend,
Jankowski

***

He read and re-read the pages a few times, then began to stare off into space. Despite being happy to send arms to Ukraine, the CIA wasn't interested in actioning intel from one of their most valuable assets. Admittedly, it had been decades since Jankowski had been active, but surely his reputation should still count for something. Even if US intelligence had shifted all its resources to focus on Islamic terrorism.

Jankowski's letter went as far as blaming the US for his death. Which meant the rest of the Five Eyes group would be equally disinterested in what he had discovered. And although they condemned Leontin in public, the French and Germans did not seem keen on any action that might provoke Russia. So who could he go to? With the exception of Ukraine, perhaps the most vocal Leontin opponents were the Poles themselves.

A few minutes later Warner was on the number 4 tram heading south towards Warsaw Chopin airport. After several stops he disembarked, skirting the sprawling buildings of the Central Hospital until he arrived outside a barbed wire-topped fence on Miłobędzka street. Behind it towered an anonymous green glass-fronted building. He stood for a moment, marvelling at the irony of what he was about to do before marching into the reception area of the Polish Foreign Intelligence Agency.

***

Later that evening, one envelope lighter, Warner was thanked for his efforts and escorted politely from the building. As he wandered back past the hospital, he finally felt as though someone was taking the issue seriously, that the Poles might actually force the USA to go after Leontin. In fact, he was so tired and relieved that he didn't notice the little man in the workers cap. And by the time he did, it was too late, he had already received a hefty shove and was falling. Falling in front of a speeding tram.

***

A few hours later Sokolov received the news from the same subordinate in the same grey conference room in the Kremlin. Neutralising Jankowski solved an immediate problem but terminating the ex-CIA agent could create another. Those sorts of "accidents" always attracted unwanted attention, even if they only involved retired agents. Just like the Russians, America still keeps tabs on their former agents and assets 'just in case'.

"Did our man in Warsaw find out what Jankowski was selling to the Americans?"

"*Nyet*, General Sokolov, the spy would tell him nothing."

"And this American, he went to the Polish security services?"

"*Da*. But we don't know what he shared - or even if the Poles took him seriously. He was an old man looking for some excitement for his boring retirement."

"Perhaps," said Sokolov doubtfully, "But I will get word to the Poles *not* to act on this information, whatever it was. We will tell them it was just an old man missing a time when he felt important. And I want you to forget all about this 'incident' too."

"Very good sir." The younger man saluted as he left.

***

The young CIA agent from Warsaw Station was quite annoyed to be awoken by his telephone ringing at 3am.

"Yes?" he demanded angrily, wiping the sleep from his eyes.

"This is the Europe Desk at Langley," said a voice, "Just a heads-up that we've analysed the material you sent over and it has been classified NFA."

"You called me in the middle of the night to tell me two old men cooked up a hooky story?"

"Yes," the voice was unapologetic, "No further

action required. NFA. Good night."

And just like that the line went dead. The young man might have been quite upset had the caller confirmed the intel was good, but instead he was relieved. NFA meant he could forget all about the overenthusiastic old man's ridiculous story. So he did.

Chapter Four

Like any big meeting involving international players, the annual NATO Summit was really for the benefit of the press. A grand affair designed to showcase the might and solidarity of the North Atlantic Treaty Organisation in an effort to prove it still has some relevance in the 21st Century. The various defence and foreign ministers of each member state sat around a circular table in a large hall in Vilnius, Lithuania, 'discussing' the situation in Ukraine and trying to formulate a unified response. The world media lapped it up, broadcasting and rebroadcasting statements from all the key players on the 24 hour news networks.

President Zelenskyy was particularly popular with the press. His statements and speeches alternated between angry threats against Russian aggression to pleading for immediate membership of NATO and the European Union for Ukraine. The 31 representatives nodded along, each careful to appear stoic and unemotional while sympathising with the plight of Ukraine. All agreed that membership could be considered at some point in the future, but careful not to make any promises. Each representative careful to ensure that they had their photos taken with the Ukrainian President, basking momentarily in his popularity.

Behind the scenes, all the usual horse-trading and

politicking was taking place, diplomatic backscratching and ego-stroking intended to keep the NATO principles happy. Similar efforts were made to strengthen the commitment of minor players so they would continue (or increase) their contributions. A trillion dollar annual budget doesn't just happen after all.

After two days of discussions, the end result was a bland statement of intent that condemned Russia's actions, promised more weapons for Ukraine and a veiled threat that NATO would be forced to take action should a member state be attacked. The statement was also very careful to confirm that Ukraine could not, and would not, be joining the North Atlantic Treaty Organisation in the near future, which was diplomatic speak for 'never'. As usual, there was nothing that would actually worry or intimidate the Kremlin.

Jankowski's revelation had been discussed in the back offices, well away from the media - and the majority of the smaller, more excitable NATO members. The intel was quickly dismissed by the Organisation's heavyweights. 'A dangerous fantasy,' claimed the US . 'A worthless, baseless rumour,' said Britain. France and Italy weren't even asked.

Mariusz Błaszyk, the Minister of National Defence of Poland had pushed back, citing the impeccable quality of Jankowski's intel in the past. Intel that the US had lapped up when it suited them. "Even if it was true, which it definitely isn't, we can't just go marching in and kill the bastard," the American representative countered, "Such an action would simply increase the scope of this war. Hell, it could even provide the excuse Leontin needs to launch a nuke at one of us. And don't go touting this bullshit to the Ukrainians either."

"But…"

"But nothing. That stunt you pulled with the Nordstream Pipeline? We don't want a repeat."

"I assure you, I know nothing of the Nordstream Pipeline sabotage."

"Of course you don't Marisuz. It's a total mystery, just some random guys in a yacht blowing up one of Europe's gas supplies, right?" The American's voice dripped with bitter sarcasm, "But any more of that bullshit and Poland will be sanctioned."

The summit ended in the usual way; attendees made a meaningless statement of unity, issued a noncommittal non-promise of potential NATO membership, smiled and shook hands for the cameras and then got the hell out of there - as far from Ukraine as they could go.

Chapter Five

The phone rang insistently, loud and annoying, echoing against the Presidential Palace walls. *Let the bastard wait*, President Andrzej Dudka thought, allowing the noise to continue for another thirty seconds. Satisfied that he would have sufficiently annoyed the caller, he lifted the receiver to his ear, "Yes?"

"Mr President? This is the President, Joe. I trust you are well?"

"Yes, Mr President, I am well. What can I do for you?"

"I wanted to follow up on the story coming from Warsaw. The Leontin rumour."

"I hear that the CIA has already dismissed the *intel*," said Dudka, emphasising the word "'The fantasies of an old man who misses the Cold War' they tell me."

"Yes, that's right," Blyden agreed, "Nothing of substance at all. I just wanted to make it clear that we won't be taking any further action. And nor will you." The caller sounded old and distant, like he was only partially engaged.

"Are you certain, Mr President?" Dudka could feel his anger, and voice, rising, "Can you really take that risk? Have you forgotten that International Criminal Court has issued an arrest warrant for this man?"

"We're certain it's nothing, Andrzej. Leave it alone. America will not take any action, Poland will not take any action. This issue ends now. We can't take any more risks, especially since the pipeline incident." Suddenly the weakness in his voice was gone, Blyden's own anger coming through loud and clear.

"Yes Mr President," he sputtered before slamming the phone down and uttering a howl of rage. He smashed the receiver on his desk a few more times for good measure. After a minute of deep breathing he picked up the phone again, "Julia, I want Błaszyk in my office the moment he flies in from Vilnius. And Kamiński too. In here. As soon as possible."

**

"I tried Andrzej. I tried the Americans and the Brits but none of them would go for it."

Dudka looked across his desk at the Deputy Prime Minister who was reclining on a sofa. With his loosened tie, creased suit and black-circled eyes, Błaszyk looked like a man who had just completed a marathon two day summit. "Of course not.," he sneered, "Blyden seems to think we'd trigger World War 3 if we went in. The old coward doesn't seem to realise it's already started."

"But how sure are you that the intel is good? I mean the guy was ex-SB. We've received word from other back channels that he was a grifter, selling lies and outdated intelligence to make a quick buck. Could he have been playing double-agent?" Mariusz Kamiński, Co-ordinator of Special Forces, cautioned.

"According to the CIA, he's never been wrong before. Everything he ever shared was accurate, actionable.

Real."

"So he's never been wrong but this one time the Americans don't want to know?" Błaszyk, couldn't make sense of it. Maybe he was just over-tired and not thinking straight.

"Probably because he has been out of the game for *thirty-five years*," the Foreign Intelligence Agency security chief blinked thorough his small eyeglasses hawkishly, "I've never heard of Jankowski and he's exactly who my guys should be aware of."

"It's possible Mariusz, or maybe he was just really, really good. Maybe it's a sign from God himself. Whatever the case, I really don't think we can ignore it. America is out, Britain is out, NATO is out. And if NATO is out, Ukraine will not go against them and place their future membership in jeopardy - even if it meant they would win this war. So we need to send a team to check on Leontin ourselves. And if it *is* Leontin, *we* can deal with the bastard." Warming to his topic, Dudka was now up and pacing behind his desk.

"There's too much at stake *not* to take action. Support for Ukraine is drying up, our people are tired of the conflict and the cost - but they won't forgive us if, when, Russia is back at our border." The Sejm elections were fast approaching and WiS opposition had crystallised into a coalition led by their fiercest rivals, Civitas. Polling suggested that even if he won a majority of votes, Dudka would not have enough seats to command a majority in the lower house. He would have to give up the presidency. Unless he could sway public opinion, *quickly*.

"We need resolution. Now. Because if the

opposition wins, we can expect them to hand our strategy-making capabilities to the EU. Ukraine will have fallen long before Brussels passes their first resolution and issues a statement. Even if we go on to lose the election, we have to do this. We cannot have the Russians on our border ever again."

"I understand what you are saying Andrzej, but we need deniability if we go in," Błaszyk cautioned, "We can't send regular troops. And we certainly can't admit to any involvement - even if we do pull this off."

"This is a job on foreign soil. *Hostile* foreign soil," added Kamińsky peering through the glasses perched on the end of his nose, "I don't think there's enough deniability if something goes wrong. Do you really think we can find private contractors willing to take this suicide mission on?"

"What about the WOT? Could we use them? They are fully trained by us and committed to the Republic of Poland. But if the mission went bad, we could claim it was just from some overenthusiastic part-time volunteers? A rogue guerrilla unit?" suggested Błaszyk.

Outside Poland, the Wojska Obrony Terytorialnej, WOT, had been treated as something of a joke when the government first announced its formation in 2017. Now the Territorial Defence Force was an army of 50,000 volunteers assembled to face down a potential threat from Russia in the East. *Not so funny now*, thought Dudka, smiling grimly to himself, "This is almost certainly our last chance to end this war and the threat from Russia. Can we get a team put together in time? A *good* team?"

"Good enough. Probably. Maybe. Let me see what I

can do."

***

After the meeting with the President ended, Błaszyk returned to his own office at the Ministry of Defence. Ironically, the window looked out onto the Russian Embassy and he stood for a few moments admiring the palace, complete with a small group of flag-waving pro-Ukraine demonstrators on the road outside. He snorted, reconsidering the madness of what he had just suggested - sending a guerrilla team into the heart of Russia to kidnap Vladimir Leontin and return him to Poland for prosecution. *Insanity*, he thought, *best to kick this over to the WOT - and fast.*

Resisting the urge to fall asleep, he picked up the phone on his desk, hoping the Russian bastards next door couldn't hear and dialled the extension for Brigadier General Maciej Kliszcz, Commander of Territorial Defence Forces.

***

A few floors below, Kliszcz had listened to the call in stunned silence. He had only been promoted to Commander a few months earlier but he knew a shitty job when he saw one. This was a *very* shitty job. On his way to the top, the Brigadier General had learned one important lesson though - shit rolls downhill. He took another moment to decide which of his subordinates he disliked the most, then dialled the number for General Grabowski of the 16th Lower Silesian Territorial Defence Brigade in Wrocław.

***

General Grabowski stared at his phone. The call from Warsaw had only lasted a few minutes but it had shocked him. He leant back in his chair, running a hand across his close-cropped grey military haircut.

After 40 years in the Polish army he had received plenty of insane orders from the higher-ups. The communists had constantly drilled him to prepare for an attack by the capitalists from the west who wanted to infect his country with their filthy decadent ways - or to rain nuclear fire from the heavens. And after Rakowski's government fell in 1989 he had been constantly drilled to prepare for an attack by the lunatics from the east who wanted to rebuild the mighty Russian empire and take back Poland for themselves. Aside from a singular focus on constant drills, the one thing all politicians had in common was paranoia.

And now he was in charge of a brigade of volunteers, the lunacy continued. Or worsened. Which madman thought it would be a good idea to send a small team of part-time soldiers into the middle of a military superpower to kidnap their supreme leader from his own backyard? A mission that Grabowski would not even send serving *kommandos* to attempt. A mission with the potential to trigger a third world war. Kliszcz must *really* hate him.

But a presidential order is a presidential order, so the veteran set to work, identifying which of his volunteers and hobbyists may be able to do the impossible.

Chapter Six

It had been another slow day for Wojciech, just how he liked it. This was a world away from his previous life, and he wouldn't give it up for anything. He had spent hours doing odd jobs around the house until it was time to collect the kids from school. Now, he stood outside, towering over the other parents, waiting to see his girls' faces as they burst out of the school gates. Standing alone, off to one side, he nodded politely to the clustered mothers who briefly paused their gossiping to nod a polite greeting.

The main door opened and he saw his two girls holding hands and skipping together through the rush of students leaving the building. Urszula, his daughter, and Oksana had been best friends the moment since Wojciech's family had agreed to take in the orphaned Ukrainian refugee. Despite differences in language, the girls were inseparable, as close as biological twins even though they looked nothing alike. Urszula was short, with wild mousey brown hair, freckled nose and green eyes. Oksana was much taller, with striking long white blonde hair gathered into a ponytail, pale skin and blue eyes. He had no idea what would happen when the war in Ukraine finally ended but he selfishly hoped that Oksana would not be returned to her homeland.

They squealed when they saw him waiting, bright smiles lighting their faces. He grinned back, lost in the moment, chest burning with pride and joy. He bent down to gather them both in a tight embrace. Then, as they walked, the girls both chattered excitedly, telling him about their day. Urszula was rambling about the book they read during story time. In halting, broken Polish, Oksana tried to explain what she had been painting in art class. Both girls were so animated and happy, their joy so infectious, that Wojciech couldn't take it all in. He just soaked in the enjoyment, nodding, smiling and laughing at the appropriate points, one girl holding on to each of his hands as they walked and skipped home. Moments like this made it easy to appreciate why he had left the army.

He frowned as they turned the corner and he spotted a large black Mercedes parked outside his house.

"Is everything ok *tata*?" Urszula asked, noting the concern on his face.

"I'm sure it's nothing," he said, his heart falling as a uniformed soldier got out of the car to meet him.

"*Dzień dobry, pan kapitan*," the soldier said with a salute.

Wojciech returned the salute, unsmiling. His frown deepened further still when his wife's blue Renault pulled up behind the Mercedes and she jumped. Her pretty face was lined with worry, her shoulders twitching with nervous energy.

"What's going on Wojciech? Is everything alright?" she demanded animatedly, adrenalin and fear coursing through her.

"Everything is fine *pani Wojciech*," the soldier said,

turning to her, palms raised placatingly, "But your husband has just been mobilised."

"I have?"

"Yes sir, I'm afraid so. With immediate effect," the soldier answered, nodding as he turned back to face Wojciech.

"Please tell me it's not Kandahar again," Wojciech's wife demanded, tears of worry and fear streaming down her face. The two girls didn't understand what was happening, but they too burst into tears.

"I'm afraid I don't know where or what the mission is *pani Wojciech*, but I have been assured it's not Afghanistan."

"Thank God," she sighed.

"I'm so sorry *moje kochanie*," Wojciech said, gathering her up in a tight embrace, "We knew this day may come and here it is."

He motioned the two girls to join them, gathering his family in his arms and kissing each one on the top of their head. "I am so, so sorry. Urszula and Oksana, I want you to look after your mother while I am gone, ok?"

"*Tak tata*," they chorused, holding each other tightly.

"I love you all. And I will see you soon."

Wojciech followed the soldier to the waiting car, stopping to take one final look at his family huddled together, worry etched on their faces. He had always said that one day he may be called up for action, but he and his wife had assumed it would be for a humanitarian mission - helping people displaced by a flood or providing extra manpower for a state event or something. But this, this was clearly different. He sat down, closed the door and blew three kisses, one for each of the women in his life.

"This had better be bloody important," he growled at the soldier up front as the car pulled away.

Chapter Seven

Paweł sighed as another half-drunk stag party wearing matching fluorescent t-shirts stumbled and pushed their way down the stairs, into the damp and dismal underground bunker which housed the Magnum shooting range. He could smell the bitter stench of stale beer, testosterone and adrenaline wafting off the eight men as they shouted and joked with each other.

"Are you serious?" he asked his boss, "You're going to let these drunken idiots onto the range? What if they shoot someone? Or themselves?"

"They have paid for the Terminator package, Paweł. All eight of them. And if you want to get paid this month, we need these idiots' money. And let's face it, you're only here because you know your shit."

Because you know you're shit, he thought, staring hard at his manager. The group had pre-paid for the most expensive experience available. And God knows they needed the money. *He* needed the money. Child support and his ex-wife were crippling him financially - and that was before the costs of starting a new life with his girlfriend. This might be a crappy job in a crappy bunker but it was marginally better than defending a hostile local population against a vicious guerrilla force with weapons that constantly jammed because of the searing heat and dust. This group of hyperactive English fools were more likely to kill themselves than him.

"No income, no pay," his manager added unnecessarily. Without saying a word, Paweł turned on his heel and went to greet the men.

"Are you ready gentlemen?" Paweł asked with what little enthusiasm he could muster. Drunks and guns were a terrifying combination, almost worse than anything he had seen in the army.

"Yeah! Let's shoot up some shit!" The Groom yelled as the rest of his group whooped and cheered.

Paweł handed a pair of ear defenders and safety glasses to each man, waiting impatiently until they had put them on. "Now, let's go over the rules. One person at the firing line at a time - that's the red one there," he pointed. "You do not come to the firing line until I call you. Otherwise you stand there behind the yellow line." He pointed again, waiting until the men shuffled obediently backwards.

"Guns *always* point that way or at the ground," Paweł indicated up the range towards the targets, "Even if you think they are empty or you have run out of bullets, your gun points at the ground. And if you turn around and a point a gun in this direction, I will shoot you."

The men laughed as he pointed at the Glock holstered on his right hip. "I'm serious gentlemen, I *will* shoot you." His hard stare said he wasn't joking and the laughter dried up. "Now please, wait behind the yellow line while I set up. And put your ear defenders on before you forget and deafen yourselves."

"Say what?" yelled the Best Man, pointing at his covered ears.

Ha ha, hilarious. Dickhead.

Paweł took a long, heavy German MG-42 machine gun from the rack on the wall and set it on the floor, pointing towards the paper targets in the distance. He connected a belt of 7.92mm rounds, checked the loading mechanism and safety, then gestured the first man forward.

"I'm up first lads!" The Groom elbowed his way through the group, "Take a photo so I can show Stacey when I get home." He straddled the gun., one leg on each side of the barrel, energetically thrusting his pelvis backwards and forwards.

"You wish mate!" One of his mates yelled back.

"Stacey'll only be jealous, now she's seen the real thing!" another called, laughing at his own joke.

"Shut up you pricks!" the groom shouted back.

The situation was getting out of hand and Paweł was sure that someone was about to get hurt, "Gentlemen, if we could just remain calm. We're here to have fun without killing anyone."

The men continued to jeer each other as the groom laid on his front with the MG-42 in front of him. Paweł quietly talked the man through the process of arming the gun, lining up the sights and releasing the safety. The groom was about to fire when he was interrupted by a shout.

"Paweł!"

The instructor quickly re-engaged the safety and released the ammunition belt from the gun. Then he turned to see who had called. A fully uniformed officer stood behind the stag party, beckoning Paweł. Behind him, the range manager was turning red with anger.

"Oi! You can't leave. We've paid to shoot shit!" the Best Man yelled, grabbing at Paweł as he walked past. Instinctively, Paweł flicked the release on his hip holster, placing a hand on the butt of his pistol. "Take. Your. Hands. Off. Me." He growled through gritted teeth.

"OK. ok, ok. Let's calm down gentlemen," the range manager elbowed his way towards the firing line, "Unfortunately Mr Paweł has become unexpectedly unavailable, so I will be taking over your shooting session today."

The manager glared angrily at Paweł while the men cheered and whistled and clapped. Paweł turned on his heel and followed the army officer out of the bunker.

Chapter Eight

Tomasz wasn't sure exactly what it was that pushed his boss over the edge, but it must have been bad. Perhaps it was because he had been late twice this week. Or the screw-up with the monthly equipment order. Maybe it was just because Jan was a prick.

After leaving the army, Tomasz had found it hard to get work. No one wanted to hire a veteran of a war that no one supported in the first place. The medals and commendations he earned working behind enemy lines in the badlands of Afghanistan were worthless back in the real world.

So Marta, his wife, had begged her brother to give him a job. And now Jan took every opportunity to remind Tomasz of the favour, humiliating and belittling the soldier who could not provide for his family. While he had been fighting the 'War on Terror' in Afghanistan his brother had been investing heavily in telecoms, making a significant fortune in the process. The worst thing was that Jan was right - even though he was good at the job, he was also totally reliant on the generosity of his prick of a brother-in-law. And Marta never failed to remind him of that fact either which inevitably led to shouting and crying and nights spent on the living room sofa.

Now he was being humiliated again. Why else would Jan have sent him out 15 minutes before the end of shift to find a downed phone line somewhere in the arse-end of nowhere? There must be all of eight people living in the village affected by this broken cable. The dickhead probably thought he was doing Marta a favour, keeping her boorish, ex-military husband out of the house for a few extra hours.

Tomasz had had to drive this country lane twice to find before he spotted the break, the line draped limply over a tree at the side of the road. And as he climbed the cement telegraph pole, the heavens had opened. Now he sat four metres above the ground, rainwater streaming off his hard hat onto his already soaking shoulders and thighs, the damp making his fingers slippery and numb.

He shifted his weight in the harness and felt his sodden overalls squelch. Since leaving the Army he had been steadily gaining weight and now he was worried that safety rope may not hold. It wasn't that he was *fat*, but he had never been this heavy - or lazy - before.

He cursed Jan who was no doubt already home, warm and dry back in the city. And screw Marta too. Screw the job and this pissy little village and the broken cable that had interrupted their Netflix. He swore loudly as the torrential rain caused his spanner to slip, every turn of every bolt an exercise in futility. He shouted at the rain, the failing light, the fields and trees and everything else he could see. Tomasz was so enraged he didn't notice the uniformed man below until he began kicking his ladder.

The shock and fear quickly got his attention though, and Tomasz began hurling abuse at the idiot who was trying to knock him down, "Seriously man, what the…?"

"You've been mobilised," the soldier shouted up at him.

"If it's Kandahar again, you can piss right off."

"No, not Afghanistan. Now can you please hurry down and get in the car?"

"*Tak* sir," Tomasz snapped off a sarcastic salute and then threw the remaining bolts into the bushes below. *Screw you, Jan.*

Moments later he was in the back of the soldier's car, his sodden clothes leaking into the upholstery and creating a cold puddle of discomfort. Then there was nothing but his abandoned works van parked up on the grass in the lonely country lane.

Chapter Nine

The light rain had been falling for hours and Adam was now soaked to the skin, his camouflaged fatigues heavy and sodden. Despite his discomfort he remained statue still, laying behind a mossy tree trunk, water puddling in the leaves and twigs around his legs. He had been here for hours now, stuck in the same position, watching, waiting.

The forest above him offered little protection from the rain but was doing an excellent job of blocking daylight. The air was thick and grey, his steaming breath adding to the mist and making it even harder to see through the gloom. He removed his sodden cap, wiping the rain from his steel grey eyes, shifting weight slightly in the hope of getting blood flowing back to his frozen toes. The ground squelched beneath him, mud oozing through his camouflaged combat trousers and matting in his bushy brown beard.

Finally he saw movement ahead, the briefest flash of white among the trees, a few hundred metres from where he lay. He craned forward, bringing his eye level to the rifle scope in front of him, then slowly scanned the space ahead until he spotted the 16-point antlers of the monarch stag he had been hunting for the past week.

He took a moment to admire the magnificent beast,

holding his breath as it turned and looked straight towards him. Hunter and hunted stared at each other for a moment before Adam began to gently pull on his trigger.

The silence was shattered by the sound of a helicopter, travelling fast at treetop level. Panicked, the stag turned and prepared to bolt just as Adam pulled the trigger. The stag flinched and his shot went high, piercing the shoulder. Bellowing in pain, the beast stumbled briefly, then fled into the trees before he could aim again. Adam snatched his rifle and vaulted the trunk, his long, lanky legs almost collapsing under him as circulation returned. Ignoring the pain he charged in the same direction, following the sound of the injured animal as it crashed through the forest.

After a moment he could see the stag, sprinting towards a clearing. The animal was still moving quickly but erratically, clearly hurt, huge clouds of breath hanging in the damp air. The sound of the helicopter was getting louder too and as the hunter broke clear of the trees he could see why. The bug-like form of an army Mi-2 sat in the centre of the clearing, its spinning rotors flattening the grass around it, while a soldier scanned the area with his binoculars. When he spotted Adam, the man waved, beckoning him towards the helicopter.

Trapped between Adam and the helicopter, blinded by fear and pain, the stag was slowing until it finally collapsed on its knees. The hunter moved forwards until he stood over the buck, its laboured breaths clouding around his regal antlers.

"*Kapral Adam,*" a voice boomed through a bullhorn, "*Kapral Adam,* we must speak immediately."

Ignoring the helicopter, Adam knelt down beside the deer and stroked its nose gently. He made quiet shushing noises, trying to calm the dying animal, hoping it would somehow understand his respect.

"*Kapral Adam*, I have orders from General Grabowski, you have been mobilised. You must come with us, *now*."

Standing up, Adam sighed, sliding the rifle bolt to chamber another round. Taking careful aim, he fired once, ending the stag's suffering. Then he turned and strode angrily towards the waiting helicopter.

Chapter Ten

Despite being an adult and a priest, Father Mateusz was popular with the younger members of his congregation. He sat with a group of teenagers, at the weekly youth group meeting.

"I wasn't born a priest you know," he said, looking at each youngster in turn, "In fact when I was your age, my priest said I was destined for Hell."

The teens laughed as he shrugged comically.

"No, it's true. I did it all. Drinking, drugs, sex. All the things that guarantee damnation. Oh, and I was also a talented car thief - until I was arrested."

The teens laughed again. Surely not Father Mateusz? He was short and slightly tubby, hair balding faster than it greyed. And he had a smiling face with twinkling, trustworthy blue eyes. The man prayed all the time, was caring, gave his time and attention and love to anyone who needed it. Their mothers loved him. He was most certainly not a common street criminal.

"So what happened?" One of them asked.

"I went to court. I was found guilty. But my priest spoke on my behalf, he pleaded for mercy. So the judge offered me a choice - jail or the army."

Mateusz was enjoying himself now, the teenagers

completely shocked by these revelations.

"Simple choice, yes? The army was great, I loved it! Until I was sent to Afghanistan," he paused thoughtfully for moment, "It turns out my priest was right - I was destined for Hell because Kandahar *was* Hell. But like many soldiers, that was where I met God."

"I vowed that if I got out of Afghanistan alive, I would devote my life to God, I would become a priest. I prayed a lot in Kandahar, even in the middle of the fiercest firefights. I prayed so often my comrades started calling me Ksiądz. When I finally came home and was still breathing I enrolled in seminary. And now I am here, trying to help you all find your way - without going to Hell."

The teenagers laughed again, but there was a new respect for the man who sat with them.

As the conversation continued, Mateusz saw the door at the back of the hall open and a young soldier stepped in.

"Have you come to tell us about your battlefield conversion, *starzy sierżant*?"

"Uh... *nie*," the soldier said, blushing as the room turned to look at her, "But we must speak *starszy szeregowy* Mateusz."

The youths turned back to Mateusz, open-mouthed.

"Are you still a soldier?" they asked.

"In the Territorial Defence Force, *tak*."

"Wow!" there was a buzz of excitement.

"Anyway, let's finish there tonight. Have a good week and I will see you soon."

"*Do widzenia!*" the youths chorused, chattering loudly about the Priest's revelations.

Father Mateusz turned his attention back to the Sergeant, "*Tak?*"

"I have orders from General Grabowski," she replied apologetically, "You have been mobilised Mateusz. Now."

"We have to leave right now?"

"Now. And you're going to be away for a few days. Now if you follow me to the car, we need to leave ASAP."

Dazed, Father Mateusz followed the Sergeant out to a waiting car still dressed in his black cassock.

Chapter Eleven

It had been a feverish 24 hours following the unexpected call from Brigadier General Kliszcz, and General Grabowski was satisfied with his efforts. He leaned back in his chair and permitted himself a tight-lipped smile. The Territorial Defence Force may be staffed by volunteers, but that doesn't mean they are incompetent amateurs. In fact, he was fiercely proud of the men and women who served under him - and he was convinced that they would all give their lives in the defence of Poland if required. But the team he selected were all former enlisted soldiers, having served a brutal tour in Afghanistan together with the JW Komandosów special reconnaissance unit before returning to civilian life. And each man could speak passable Russian too.

Grabowski leaned forward and looked at the five manila folders on his desk, service records of five good men who had served under him and trusted him. And now he would soon be sending them into enemy territory. Five men who thought they had finished active duty, who had more than earned their return to civilian life. He idly flicked through each file one final time, sighing. He was sending five of his very best into Russia on a suicide mission.

Chapter Twelve

Grabowski stood outside the briefing room, watching the men carefully to see how they interacted, whether they were still a team.

"So tell me again Ksiądz," Tomasz was speaking loudly to Mateusz, "How can a priest be a soldier?"

"Who says a priest can't be a soldier?" Ksiądz parried.

"God. God says."

"Does He?"

"Yes, in the Bible."

"Where?"

"You know, in the Ten Commandments. 'Thou shalt not kill'."

"Are you sure that's what it says? You don't want to check?" The grinning priest tossed his comrade a pocket-sized Bible.

"No Ksiądz, I'm sure," Tomasz threw the book back.

"You should have checked man. It says 'Thou shalt not *murder*'. And I've never murdered anyone."

"Oh."

The rest of the team fell about laughing, eventually joined by Tomasz too. "Don't worry Ksiądz, I'll still let you pray for us," he grinned.

Pleased with what he saw, Grabowski walked into the briefing room. "Gentlemen, it's been a while, but it's good to see you all again."

"*Tak panie generał!*" the men saluted.

"Let me start by apologising for the rush to get you here. I am particularly sorry that some of you were unable to say goodbye to your loved ones before being dragged down here," Grabowski was genuinely regretful, knowing that the men needed to make proper farewells if they were to focus fully on the task in hand. Especially given the ridiculous dangers involved with this mission, "However time is of the essence and there's not a minute to spare. I will make sure that you have time to call your families this evening."

"Just one question sir," Tomasz said, raising his hand like a schoolboy, "It's not Kandahar again, is it?"

"No gentlemen, you will be pleased to hear it's not Kandahar."

All of the men sighed with relief. Nothing could be as bad as a return trip to Afghanistan, surely?

"But now, let's get down to business. Obviously you all know each other and what you're capable of. And I'm sure you already know what role you'll play in this team. But then you've all been out of the force for a while so maybe you've forgotten how it works," Grabowski said with a grin, "Wojciech, you're in charge so it's your job to make sure this bunch gets the job done. Paweł, you'll do weapons. Tomasz on comms and Ksiądz will take care of transport. Adam, you will supply firepower support."

"'Do weapons'?" Asked Paweł, "What does that

mean? Are we going into a mission unarmed?"

"This one is a little... *different*," said Grabowski. The moment of reckoning had arrived when the General would have to explain what expected his men to do. He felt slightly sick.

"Different? Different *how*?" As should be expected of a leader, Wojciech was concerned about what they were being ordered to do, "What have you got us into?"

Grabowski respected the man's sense of responsibility, "A mission of national importance. Maybe you even pull the rest of the world away from the brink too."

"Right," laughed Adam drawing the word out sarcastically.

"You're going into Russia."

"To kill Leontin?" Tomasz suggested. The team began to laugh.

"*Nie*. You're going to exfiltrate Leontin. Alive."

It took several minutes for the roaring laughter to die down. Grabowski stood smiling silently, enjoying the moment with his men. But eventually they realised he was serious and the atmosphere in the room changed. Grabowski hadn't been lying, this mission was going to be very, very different. The churning in his stomach wasn't getting any better.

"Whether they expect it to be served or not, the International Criminal Court has issued an arrest warrant for Leontin. Obviously he won't be crazy enough to set foot in a country that recognises the ICC - he's effectively gone into hiding in Russia. So we're going to have to go in and get him."

"And get out again," Ksiądz said in a mock whisper to the rest of the team.

"Yes, and out again," Grabowski agreed, "We have a plan that will get you in and out. Obviously it's ridiculously dangerous, but I - we - think your team might just pull it off."

"At least the weather should be better than Kandahar," said Tomasz to another gale of laughter.

***

Normally, Grabowski would have had weeks or months to prepare his team for a covert operation behind enemy lines. This time he had mere hours. Given that the men had not seen active duty for several years, he was impressed by their relative levels of fitness and the way they had stepped back into military life almost immediately. He wouldn't say the men were fully combat-ready, but at least they stood a fighting chance. As a team they had managed to run a few kilometres carrying fully-laden kitbags, doing laps outside the long, red brick barracks. No one had coughed up a lung or dropped dead and they had all worked together, so there was hope for them as a team. Drills on the firing range with confiscated Russian weaponry were similarly successful, they could all still shoot straight too. Clearly the twice yearly training camps organised for members of the WOT were having the desired effect, creating an army of reservists with genuine combat skills.

Using the short amount of time available, Grabowski concentrated on the plan, such as it was.

"Obviously we can't enter Russian airspace, so we can't parachute you in. A crossing via Belarus is out of the question given their political alliance with Moscow and the fact we are currently reinforcing our shared border. Transiting via Kaliningrad is too risky, there's simply too many variables, not least how to cross a heavily militarised, closed border. That leaves Ukraine."

"Ukraine? You want us to pass through the front line?" Wojciech was shocked.

"*Tak*. You'll enter Ukraine here at Korczowa," Grabowski pointed to a spot on the map that was spread across the table in front of them, "You'll be travelling as civilians, driving across country to meet with a contact from the local Azov regiment here in Kharkiv." He jabbed another point on the map, several hundred kilometres to the east. "Paweł, tell me the weaponry you need and Azov will have it ready for you. But please remember, we want this mission to be as low-key and quiet as possible."

"*Dobrze kapitan*," the weapons specialist set to work drawing up a kit list.

Grabowski turned his attention back to Wojciech, swiping a finger across the map as he spoke, "Once armed you will be shown where to cross the border into Russia, south of Belgorod. Then it's up to you to get the team to the final destination, here"

Wojciech whistled. There was a lot of ground to cover.

"It doesn't matter how you get there, but you must be in place by the morning of April 27," Grabowski laboured the point, "Four days from now, April 27th. If you're late, we lose our chance to grab Leontin. Probably forever."

"April 27," Wojciech echoed, "We'll be there General."

Grabowski and Wojciech went over the plan, rehearsing various timings and waypoints, looking for potential problems and improvements. They examined every inch of the Dolgiye Borody peninsula, discussing entry and exit points and how to transport a hostage out of Russia and back to a friendly country without attracting attention. Wojciech thought plan was quite mad - but that was also its genius.

Meanwhile the rest of the team were drilled endlessly about their cover stories and fake identities that they would never use. They even had a few hours with a linguist, helping to develop passable Russian accents.

Much to his disgust, Adam was forced to shave off his beard. "Facial hair is forbidden in the Russian Army, especially the elite units" Grabowski had warned him.

"Anyway, it just looks like a dead cat glued to your face," Tomasz had added unhelpfully. The hunter had said nothing himself, merely uttered a growl of anger, his flinty eyes flashing.

Despite these preparations, it didn't feel like enough to satisfy the veteran general. He felt as though all he had done was point to a random spot on a map and given them four days to get in and out of one of the most militarised nations on Earth. One that was actively involved in a war. Without backup, they would be totally alone.

He took a breath. Although technically civilians, these were highly trained, capable men. Perhaps they might just do the impossible.

Chapter Thirteen

"Come on Piotr, you knew this day was coming," the woman in the suit was stirring her coffee aggressively. Brown hair scraped back in a savage ponytail, minimal makeup, laser stare - she was all business.

"But you didn't have to come and get me at work," the young, bearded man looked like he was about to cry, "We could have met somewhere in the evening like we normally do. Now I have to explain why agents from the ABW are turning up in the office. I haven't even done anything wrong."

"Stop sniffling Piotr," the woman said, laying her spoon on the saucer and staring hard at the hacker, "You had a choice - prison time or be my pet. So when I call, you come."

Piotr sighed. She was right, he *had* made the deal. In fact, he couldn't believe his luck when the Agencja Bezpieczeństwa Wewnętrznego (ABW - Internal Security Agency) had offered to spare him prison time for hacking the Narodowy Bank Polski. Especially as he had temporarily, siphoned off more than five million zloty - before he was arrested. After his trial, all he had to do was forward useful information about the Polish hacking community to the ABW. He felt like he had won a second chance at life. But that was before he met Agent Agnieszka. She was a *bitch*.

"So what do you want?" he sighed again.

"That's better Piotr," she said with a smile, "I need an intro to NLB."

"You need *what*?"

"You heard me, NLB," she nodded, anticipating his next question, "the Ukrainians. And I need you to set it up, fast."

"I think they are a little busy at the moment," Piotr snarked, "There's a war going on, haven't you heard?"

"Now, now Piotr, there's no need to be like that," Agent Agnieszka tutted, "And you're right, there *is* a war going on. But I'm relying on you to set up a meeting. Tomorrow."

"Tomorrow? Are you crazy?"

"Yes, Piotr, we need to make contact tomorrow. I don't know who you have to talk to, I don't *care* who you have to talk to. I must have a meeting, *tomorrow*."

"But…"

"But nothing. I know about your secret laptop, hidden behind the vent in the furnace room of your tenement block. I know you're still poking around the dark web and talking with your hacker pals. And I know you know that's a violation of your agreement with the ABW. So you get online and tell them I'm offering $500,000 US for a few hours work on the 26th. Or Bitcoin or whatever it is you geeks are into. Half now, half when the job is done."

She stared hard at Piotr again, smirking. The man sank even lower in his seat.

"They'll smell a rat. The whole thing smells of feds.

Why not just use your own cyber defence teams?"

"As our American friends like to say, 'plausible deniability' Piotr. So whatever you do, make sure they don't smell *anything*. Do I have to remind you what will happen if you screw this up?"

She didn't have to, because Agent Agnieszka never missed an opportunity to remind him of the consequences of reneging on his deal. She enjoyed watching his discomfort.

"Straight to jail, Piotr. Straight. To. Jail."

She grabbed her bag and stood up, "Tomorrow Piotr. I need to make contact *tomorrow*."

And then she was gone.

Chapter Fourteen

Most of the 16th Territorial Brigade had been shipped north east to the Belarus border where a stand-off had developed between Poland and Russian-trained militia. Tensions were high, and the Polish government wanted to be ready just in case anything kicked off. Grabowski had actually been recalled from the frontline to oversee the Leontin mission.

The team had been drilled and grilled for hours, cramming as much preparation as they could into the time available. It was approaching midnight when Grabowski let them retire to their cots in an empty barracks building. Despite the late hour, each man took the opportunity to call home. Worried wives and sleepy children slurred their goodbyes and plenty of quiet tears were shed.

Wojciech spoke to his wife first and explained as much as he was allowed. It would never be enough to fully calm her, but she had been a military wife for years; she knew the drill, even if she didn't like it. He then spoke to each of the girls in turn. Urszula tried to be brave, promising to look after her mother, to make her father proud. Having already lost one father, Oksana was terrified that Wojciech may leave her too. Despite the importance of the mission, he silently cursed his luck, having assumed that he would never be called up for something like this again. He couldn't remember feeling this torn ever before, not even during the darkest days of his tour in Kandahar where death, destruction and futility were his constant companions.

Tomasz's wife, Marta, had exploded as soon as the call connected. Where the hell was he? Why did he not come home last night? Her brother Jan had called to rage about her lazy, incompetent husband and how he had simply walked away from a half-finished job. When she finally paused for breath, Tomasz was able to break the bad news. Marta immediately softened when she realised he had a good reason for his disappearance. She even offered to apologise to Jan for the dumped truck and incomplete phone line repair job. She woke their two sons, Jacek and Błażej so he could say his goodbyes and she apologised tearfully for thinking the worst of him. When they finally finished, Tomasz felt drained, almost regretting making the call in the first place.

Oliwia, Paweł's girlfriend was both angry and worried and relieved. When he hadn't come home from work she had called the shooting range, only to be told that he had been escorted away by a soldier on official business. She had rung all of his friends and family trying to find out what had happened, but no one knew anything. Had he been mobilised? Arrested? Kidnapped? So many scenarios played out in her head, none of them good. Eventually he had been able to calm Oliwia, assured her everything was alright, that he was shipping out for a few days, nothing to worry about, he would see her soon. Afterwards he made a second call to his ex-wife who agreed to wake his son Sami so he could say goodbye. The boy chattered excitedly to his father about kindergarten and his favourite toys and *matka's* new friend Adam who was living with them now. Paweł tried to concentrate on Sami, but found his mind wandering to how much of Adam's lifestyle his child support payments was funding.

Lacking a partner, Adam called his widowed mother who was just pleased to hear his voice. Her only son was a loner, keeping irregular contact, so a call like this was a precious rarity. But she knew he was a good man, trustworthy, capable and honourable - a good soldier. They chatted for a while, light, inconsequential topics, Mother simply glad to spend time with her son. Eventually Adam dropped his deployment into the conversation. He heard her breath catch as she stifled a sob, the line went silent for a moment. Then she continued chatting about the mundane minutiae of life and Adam listened, the distraction strangely comforting.

Sat on the cot in the furthest corner, Ksiądz had no one to call, no next of kin. He didn't envy his comrades, nor feel jealous of them as they made their tearful goodbyes. Instead he fingered his rosary and offered whispered prayers of protection for them all and their families. It was in these moments of tension and worry that his faith seemed to grow, giving him the energy he needed to help and support the team.

One by one the calls ended and each man climbed under his blanket. Wojciech was the last to hang up. He wasn't afraid, but he understood why his wife and daughters were frightened and he was sorry he could not be there to comfort them. He stood to extinguish the lights, taking one last look across the room at his now sleeping team mates, his second most-favourite group of people in the world.

***

Piotr had retrieved his laptop from behind the vent grating in the furnace room, just where Agent Agnisezka had said it would be. Nosey spy bitch. Probably served him right for thinking he could pull one over on the security services though. He shoved the computer into his satchel and headed back out into the night, walking quickly to the McDonalds at the end of his street. The restaurant was closed, but he was here to anonymously piggyback off their free WiFi connection, not for anything to eat. He sat down at a picnic bench in the shadows around the corner of the building and opened the laptop, firing up his Tor client.

    Once connected, Piotr navigated through layers of the dark web like he was on autopilot. After a few minutes he landed on a heavily encrypted chat server. Gaining access was a multi-stage process. First he had to type two 32 character passcodes. Then he had to connect the special hardware token that hung from a chain around his neck to the USB port on the side of his laptop. Verification complete and chatroom loaded, he watched as text began scrolling up the screen, his digital comrades and competitors greeted him; Pi-d0g was online.

Chapter Fifteen

"I've said this before, and I'm going to keep saying it," the General said, "This mission is completely unofficial. You're going in alone without any protection or cover. And if you're captured, the Polish government will not, *cannot* do anything. Everything about your mission will be denied and you will be publicly denounced."

"NATO, acts of war, foreign spies etc etc," said Wojciech, "You've said this before remember, Sir?"

The rest of the squad laughed, but the sound was hollow. The tension was ratcheting up the closer they were to moving out. This wasn't just a happy reunion any more.

"This really isn't funny," the General said, sharing a smile, "But we wish you the very best of luck. The defence chief thinks you may even be on a mission from God Almighty himself. If you manage to bring Leontin back, you just might be saving the world after all."

As the team prepared to leave, Grabowski began to feel The Fear, that unshakeable feeling of impending doom that precedes any mission. Only this time it was much, much worse because the chances of success were so slim.

The plan he had just outlined to the team was too sketchy. There were too many unknowns, too much reliance on improvisation and nowhere near enough preparation. As the team filed out of the briefing room he was forced to admit to himself that it would be a miracle if this mission got past the first 24 hours.

***

The 16th Lower Silesian Territorial Defence Brigade does not have a parade ground. So the car park at the rear of the property, behind the imposing red brick admin blocks and barracks, had become a temporary helicopter landing pad.

General Grabowski stood on a lonely island of grass and watched as the unarmed, underprepared men jogged across the damp cement, bent under the weight of their packs. They clambered into one of two waiting W-3 Sokół helicopters which would fly them to their first rendezvous point at Radymno. Grabowski smiled wryly as Ksiądz paused at the aircraft door and began splashing the fuselage with water from his flask, *Some things never change.*

The light was failing and a fine rain hung in the air, not quite heavy enough to fall but just enough to make everything wet. The carpark was deserted and the sound of the rotors echoing off the surrounding barracks and workshops was deafening.

Wojciech was the last to board, pausing for a moment on the tarmac to give his commanding officer a smart salute, a gesture his commanding officer returned solemnly. Then Wojciech was in, the door slid closed behind him and the Sokół staggered into the air. Grabowski watched as the helicopter wobbled slightly before powering off into the gathering darkness.

Satisfied that the team were out of sight and the mission properly under way, Grabowski walked quickly towards the other helicopter which would fly him north to the Mission Control centre in Warsaw.

Chapter Sixteen

Every mission begins with excitement, but as they left Radymno in an unmarked minibus and neared the Ukraine border, the mood became heavier. *Like a funeral shroud weighing us down*, thought Wojciech. The joking and banter dried up with every passing mile.

There was a steady stream of traffic travelling in the opposite direction, buses full of tear-streaked women and children trying to escape the fighting back home. Each vehicle would unload its cargo of human misery, before returning to the border for another load. In the meantime, the refugees would be dispersed throughout Poland, welcomed into the homes of ordinary men and women who genuinely wanted to help Leontin's helpless victims.

There was also a large troop build-up along the border. *NATO fools with their big talk, posing for the cameras*, Wojciech smiled to himself, *and Leontin knows that they would continue to do absolutely nothing, even if he drove up to the border himself.*

Paweł pointed at a UK unit leaning idly against their Ocelot armoured vehicle, "Those tossers wouldn't do anything if the Russian tanks just kept on coming over the line and into Poland."

"I think I've heard that story before," agreed

Tomasz sarcastically.

"I guess we're about to find out if NATO membership actually counts for anything," growled Adam. "Now if you would please shut up, this might be the last shut-eye we get for a few days and I intend to make the most of it."

The team laughed, even though he was right.

"He's still upset about losing the beard," Ksiądz whispered with a wink.

***

Because of the secrecy of the mission, the team could not afford to be seen by anyone, not least because they each carried a Russian Ground Forces uniform in their pack. Instead of a bunk in a barrack they were given the corner of a warehouse currently being used to store charity aid. The brand new, pre-fabricated metal building was overflowing with cardboard boxes of blankets and clothing stacked floor to ceiling, along with pallets of dried food and sacks of rice. The team found themselves a small space of unused concrete floor in one of the furthest corners.

"Brilliant," Ksiądz muttered sarcastically as Adam dropped his pack, unlaced his boots and threw himself on to the floor, ready to sleep, "But don't put your stinking feet near my face." Adam grinned back, waggling his toes.

"Keep your heads and noise down tonight please," cautioned Wojciech, "Remember, we're not *here*."

It was cold and uncomfortable, but they all knew far worse awaited them tomorrow. "Still better than Kandahar," said Tomasz, as he pulled his cap over his eyes.

***

Unsurprisingly, there was no queue to cross the border into

Ukraine, especially not at the crack of dawn. No one in their right mind heads *into* a war zone. The Polish border guards examined their paperwork and looked suspiciously at the fuel cans stacked in the back of the ancient Renault Espace they had been given as they left the warehouse. Once across the no man's land gap between fences, the Ukrainians simply waved them on without a second glance.

"And that, my friends, was the end of the easy part," said Wojciech, "Now the real work begins. Time to turn your trackers on."

Each man pressed the power button on the small satellite tracker unit that sat snugly in his armpit.

***

"They've just gone live, sir," announced the operator back at mission control in Warsaw, pointing at five red dots on the large satellite map overlay being projected onto the wall. "They are crossing the Ukrainian border right on schedule."

"And so it begins gentlemen, so it begins" said Grabowski dialling a number on his cellphone. "They're on their way," he said when the call connected.

"And how long until they reach the next crossing point?" asked Błaszyk.

"Approximately 24 hours if they stay on schedule, sir."

"I will see you tomorrow then General."

"Very good sir," Grabowski hung up and settled into the chair that he wouldn't leave for the next three days. The dots continued to inch slowly into Ukraine.

Chapter Seventeen

It was just after eight when Piotr called the voicemail service used by Agent Agniseszka.

"It took all night, but it's done. 1pm today," he said, "Call me."

He was on the bus to work when she did.

"I'll pick you up from your office at lunch," she was brusque, sounded distracted, "Tell your boss you need the afternoon off work."

"But.."

But she was gone.

***

The roads in the western part of Ukraine were in surprisingly good condition. There was plenty of traffic heading west and very little serious damage to bridges or highways. Yet.

Ksiądz was making good time, clearing Lviv well before midday. "Only another 1500 kilometres to the front line," he said, grinning, "Which one of you bastards wants to drive after lunch?"

***

Agent Agnieszka had driven Piotr back to his flat and followed him in, not waiting for an invite. He slammed the door behind her, and yawned.

"Don't start Piotr, we don't have time. Let's get this meeting started, yes?"

He sighed and began the complicated process of joining the dark web once more.

"You do know we have a copy of your hardware key, don't you?" She asked with malicious glee.

Piotr clenched his jaw, grinding his teeth, refusing to be baited in his own home.

"OK, they're here," he said after a few minutes of clicking and clacking, "Now what?"

"Now we tell them what they have to do on the 27th," she rolled her eyes.

***

It was a hard 12 hour drive to Kharkiv, with occasional stops to refuel and change driver. As they approached the edges of the city it was clear they were entering a war zone. Piles of rubble lined the streets while high rise apartment blocks leaned crazily after sustaining rocket strikes and artillery fire. Every now and then a haunted face would peer out of the shadows, a local scavenging for food, water or something to burn to stay warm.

Ksiądz had resumed driving duties and Wojciech was directing him towards their first rendezvous. Up ahead they could see a jeep parked next to two burned out cars. A soldier leaned against the jeep, smoking casually. "I'd say that's our contact," said Wojciech nodding towards the man. Ksiądz brought the MPV to a stop just short of the soldier and Wojciech opened his door. "Wait here," he told the rest of the team before turning his attention to the waiting man, "*Dobry vecher.*"

"*Dobry vecher* Polish," said the soldier, showing a

set of yellow, broken teeth, "You need help getting into Russia, yes? Crazy Polish."

He laughed, shaking his large, bearded head in disbelief. The man looked like a bear.

"I am Gennady. Come Polish. First some rest, then I take you."

Chapter Eighteen

The NLB members were in uproar following the virtual meeting with Pi-d0g. The encrypted IRC channel was on fire as they discussed what was on offer, what was required and whether to accept.

***

>> Who the hell is this Pi-d0g guy?
>> How do we know this isn't a scam by Russian cybersecurity?
>> Pi-d0g is legit. Can vouch.
>> Yup, Polish legend
>> If he's so good, why can't he do it himself??
>> Yea, good q. Y not?
>> He didn't say. But 500K is 500K
>> Half a million dollars, just to take down mobile communications in
    one area for a few hours? Easy money.
>> Too easy
>> Can we afford to divert resources away from the war?
>> Can we afford not to?
>> 500000 sounds good
>> ^^^ this
>> Where target?
>> Some area north of Moscow
>> Why?
>> WHY??? WHAT IS THERE??
>> Who is Pi-d0g fronting?
>> Don't know. But he's ok

\>\> Sounds sketchy
\>\> derp
\>\> He wants a cell service disrupted, dumbass. Of course it's sketchy
\>\> :D
\>\> Best approach?
\>\> Cut down local cell towers?
\>\> Ha ha
\>\> Unless you're planning a trip to Russia, no. Any serious   suggestions?
\>\> DDoS carpetbomb
\>\> Carpetbomb
\>\> Botnet carpetbomb with cycling payloads
\>\> Yes, this ^^
\>\> OK, so we're doing this?
\>\> Yes
\>\> Yea
\>\> HELL YEAH!!
\>\> I'm in
\>\> Then it's on

***

It would be a long night as the disparate, desperate group planned how to engineer a sophisticated cyberattack that would need to launch in a matter of days.

***

There was something very disconcerting about being unarmed but so close to the frontline of an active war. The rattle of small arms fire and field artillery tore through the night, the sounds getting closer the further the group walked. The five Poles had followed Gennady quickly and quietly, darting from shadow to shadow as they made their way out the northern side of the ruined city.

After marching what felt like several kilometres, the Ukrainian soldier had brought them to a roofless barn, its rough stone walls mangled and bent by shelling. There was nothing but a large gap where the door should have been.

"Taken for firewood last winter," Gennady explained, "Same with the hayloft and roof rafters."

Empty metal stalls lined the opposite wall, damp straw spilling out of the open gates. The warehouse of the previous night had been luxurious in comparison to the digs offered by the Azov Regiment. Lacking its wooden supporting structure, the barn looked as though it could collapse inwards at any moment. It certainly did not look like a major arms depot for the region.

At the far end of the open barn floor, two soldiers sat with their backs to the wall next to a stack of ammunition crates and assorted weaponry. They eyed the Poles suspiciously until Gennady gave them a reassuring nod. Satisfied there was no threat, they returned their attention to a field radio, which hissed and crackled like an angry snake at their feet.

Gennady pointed at one of the stalls where a khaki green canvas had been tied across the top to providing some shelter from the angry sky above, "That is your room tonight Polish."

"Still better than Kandahar," Tomasz muttered.

"Maybe tonight you get lucky Polish," Gennady was laughing again, a loud, booming noise that matched his bear-like stature, "Maybe President Leontin puts on a special rocket show for you"

"I bloody hope not," muttered Paweł, tossing his pack into the stall.

"But first, I have gifts," Gennady's smile grew even wider, "Russia's finest."

Four AK-12 assault rifles fitted with suppressors stood against the wall and several spare magazines. He snatched up several webbed holsters from the top of the ammunition crates, tossing each of the Poles an MP-443 Grach pistol.

"Oh, yes!" Paweł was much happier now. He picked up one of the rifles, checked the slide and sighted along the barrel, "Oh *yes*."

"Good?" Asked Wojciech.

"*Very*," Paweł grinned.

"And someone needs this too?" Gennady was holding an SVDM sniper rifle.

"*Spasibo*," nodded Adam.

"Radios, suppressors, more ammunition and another special toy in the pack there too. So, vodka then sleep, *da*?" laughed Gennady, reaching for his hip flask.

"*Da!*" They were all laughing together now.

Adam shouldered the SVDM and walked towards the door, "I'll join you in a few minutes. I just need a little practice to make sure I can actually hit something with this."

***

Once outside Adam could see mortar and rocket fire flashing in the not-too-distant north. He moved stealthily in that direction, pausing in the ruins of a bombed-out cottage. Tracer rounds arced like droplets of green fire from the Russian side of the front line, helping him to locate the shooter's position.

He knelt down in the rubble, unshouldered the SVDM and balanced its bipod legs on the remains of the cottage wall as a rest. He hadn't used one of these Russian-made rifles in many years, but the ugly folding stock and extra long barrel were still surprisingly familiar. Squinting through the sight he made a few adjustments, following the tracer fire back to its source. He focused and refocused until he could see the shooter, the tracer fire briefly illuminating the soldier's face with each barium-tipped round.

His range finder put the shooter at least 1100 metres away, nearing the upper limit of the rifle's capabilities. But it would be a good test of the gun and his mastery of it.

He chambered his first round, centred the illuminated reticule on his target's upper torso, exhaled and squeezed the trigger. There was a roar and a flash as the bullet erupted from the barrel. The rifle's built in flash suppressor had done its job, preventing him from being night-blinded, so he immediately rescanned the target area through his scope. The bullet had missed, striking the tree a few inches right and down from the shooter's body. The shooter himself was hurriedly scanning the trees and bushes opposite, trying to spot who was targeting him. Adam watched as the rifle scanned left, then double-backed as the Russian spotted him hidden behind the crumbling wall and began lining up his own return shot.

Adam adjusted his scope slightly then repeated the routine. Chamber, aim, breathe, fire. This time he could see the soldier lying on the ground, writhing in pain. Adam studied his movements until he could confirm the bullet had struck the man fatally somewhere in the gut. He made another small adjustment then took a third and final shot, this time on target. His bullet hit the man in the centre of the chest, killing him instantly.

Satisfied, Adam re-shouldered the SVDM and crept back to his comrades at the ruined barn. He hoped they had saved him sip of vodka.

***

"Yes?" Agent Agnieszka asked groggily, the phone call had clearly roused her from a deep sleep.

Piotr grinned with sadistic pleasure - it was nice to get his own back on her for once. "It's on," he said, and then hung up before she could reply. He turned his phone off so she couldn't call back and went to bed himself.

"Bastard geek," she muttered when her return calls to Piotr failed to connect. She sighed and dialled the Warsaw number she had been given by her boss. Sure enough, it went through to an anonymous voicemail box like she herself used. She sighed, "It's on."

The she hung up and buried her head under the pillow, willing herself back to sleep.

Chapter Nineteen

It was just after 3am when Gennady woke them, "Come Polish, we go now. Quick, quiet please."

The team grabbed their packs and weapons, falling into a line behind Gennady as they exited the ruins of the barn. The weather had improved somewhat while they slept, a light breeze chasing away the clouds, leaving the countryside bathed in a silvery moonlight glow. Looking behind, Wojciech could see the outlines of the shattered city, smashed buildings rising from the darkness appeared as black voids in the inky night sky. Ahead there were occasional flashes, as Ukrainian and Russian soldiers traded artillery shells and more tracer fire.

"Perhaps you tell me what your mission is, eh Polish?" Gennady asked Paweł.

Wojciech shot him a warning glance.

"Oh, you know, freelance reconnaissance," Paweł deflected.

"'Freelance reconnaissance'?," Gennady scoffed, "NATO would not cross the Russian border."

"We are not NATO," Wojciech cut in, "We are not soldiers. We work alone."

"Sure, crazy Polish," Gennady pretended to be offended before breaking into a laugh, "You keep your secrets then."

After following a country track for a kilometre or so, Gennady gave a low, slow whistle. An answering whistle came from ahead and two shadowy figures emerged from a foxhole on their right. They traded a few whispered words with Gennady eyeing the men suspiciously. Whatever Gennady said, it had the desired effect and the men were quickly ushered past the observation post. Wojciech nodded a silent greeting to the sentries, noting the tired, worn faces of men who have been at war for too long.

The further they went, the more scarred and damaged the landscape became. Tank tracks and shell craters had gouged the earth, spent bullet casings glinted in the moonlight. They moved slowly and soundlessly through the uneven terrain hoping that their progress was not being observed.

Eventually Gennady stopped at the edge of some scrubby bush. He gestured Wojciech to join him at the front of the group. Pointing into the darkness ahead, "Five hundred metres and you cross the line. You go that way Polish. *Quiet.*"

"Is it mined?" asked Wojciech.

Gennady shrugged and grinned, "Maybe. Probably. Who knows? Crazy Russians!"

"OK lads, last chance to pull out. Anyone want to go home?" Wojciech whispered to his men. He looked at each in turn, noting their silent head shakes.

"Fine, then it's time to change and get moving. Let's do this."

Gennady eyed each man in turn, nodded in approval and then grabbed Wojciech in a bear hug, "*Udachi* Polish, *udachi.*" Then he quickly turned and melted silently back into the shadows, leaving the men alone in the dark.

When he was sure the Ukrainian was gone, Wojciech spoke quietly, "Time to get dressed."

Each man quickly changed into the Russian Ground Forces uniform carried in his pack, replacing them with his civilian clothes.

"We look pretty sharp," Tomasz said, his grinning teeth shining in the dark.

"OK, let's move," Wojciech whispered.

"*Da kapitan*," they chorused.

***

Adam took up a firing position, scanning no man's land for potential hazards. Satisfied there weren't any surprises waiting for the team, he nodded to his captain, "I'll cover you all on the way across to those trees over there. You can return the favour when it's my turn. And try not to stand on any mines, ok?"

"I knew all that practice we had dodging IEDs in Afghanistan would come in handy one day," said Tomasz sarcastically.

Wojciech gestured the other three men forwards into the imaginary gap between Ukrainian and Russian forces, following closely behind. Paweł led the way, using his rifle barrel to slowly sweep the area in front of his feet. Crouching low to the ground the other men travelled quickly as possible across the exposed, silent stretch of battle-scarred field, treading softly to avoid triggering any anti-personnel devices. After a few hundred metres Paweł raised his hand and the men behind stopped.

"There's something here," he whispered, pointing at

the ground just in front of him. Wojciech squinted where indicated, spotting a fine line glimmering in the moonlight, stretched slightly where Adam's barrel had caught against it. The line passed across the track, about ten centimetres above the ground, almost completely hidden by the grass and scrub. Tomasz and Ksiądz each knelt down, taking covering positions while Paweł ran a finger carefully along the tripwire, "I think it's a bounding mine. Don't anybody move."

Wojciech shivered. Once tripped, a small charge would throw the mine into the air where it would explode. The cast iron casing would fragment into thousands of pieces, obliterating everything within 25 metres. They would all die - and probably not instantly.

"Can you disarm it?"

"Maybe, if I haven't already triggered it. Let's hope it's not booby-trapped to prevent mine clearing."

Over the pounding of his own heart, Wojciech could hear Ksiądz begin a hurried, whispered prayer somewhere in the darkness to his right.

Maintaining the same amount of pressure on the line, Paweł bent down, painfully slowly. He stroked the silver thread carefully looking for any sign of secondary devices. He paused for a long moment then seemed to make up his mind. In one slow, gentle motion he snipped the line with a pair of pliers. The wire fell harmlessly to the ground and he let out a sigh of relief. Wojciech gasped and wiped his forehead on his sleeve; in the tension of the moment he had forgotten to breathe.

Satisfied the mine had been dealt with, Paweł resumed his careful shuffle towards the Russian frontline.

Despite being just a few hundred metres, to seemed to take an age before they reached the cover of the trees opposite. Once safely across, each man turned and knelt, pointing his rifle back the way he had come. Moments later, Adam appeared from the darkness to join them.

"What took you so long? Paweł forget to tie his bootlaces again?" he joked.

"Seriously not funny man," said Tomasz, still somewhat shaken. Wojciech wasn't in the mood for joking either, so he motioned silently for the group to move forward, deeper into Russian territory.

Over the next few hours they would follow a small stream heading north, until it split in two. They would then take the right-hand branch for approximately eight kilometres as it weaved eastwards towards another tiny village, S Vergilevka - or whatever remained of it after being shelled by Ukrainian forces.

***

Huddled in a tiny bunker, two metres below ground, Private Ivanov, a signals specialist, had been awoken by the soft bleeping of the infrared detection array. He scrambled out of his sleeping bag and felt his boot sinking into the soft mud below. Hastily constructed during a lull in hostilities, his underground monitoring station was slowly flooding. As the water rose, the unlined earthen walls were becoming weaker. Eventually they would collapse inwards, crushing whichever poor bastard was on duty at the time. But being buried alive may be better than returning to the Vergilevka camp and its motley crew of murderers, rapists and violent criminals.

He squelched a few steps to the unfinished wooden

plank which served as a workbench so that he could check the tiny screen displaying the feed from the infrared monitoring cameras above. Shining out of the darkness, there was a group of white blobs that were vaguely human in shape.

At least it's not bloody rabbits triggering the system again.

It looked like a forward scouting party - but were they Russian or Ukrainian, coming or going? He slung his rifle over his shoulder and grabbed a pair of night vision glasses that were hanging from a nail driven into the cracked earthen wall before scrambling up a short wooden ladder. At the top he slowly and quietly lifted a metal hatch, allowing him to peek out across no man's land. In the distance he could see a group of five men moving stealthily towards the Wagner camp to the north. They were clearly wearing the uniform of the Russian Ground Forces, but there was something odd about them.

Probably more of those Wagner dogs deserting. Or some cheeky Ukrainian bastards getting bolder. Whoever it was didn't matter. All he had to do was radio in *any* movements in the area - it was up to the brass to decide what to do with his intel.

Once the men had disappeared from sight, he gently lowered the hatch and climbed back down into the grave-like bunker. He radioed divisional headquarters and gave them a quick description of what he had seen, *their problem now*. Then he settled back into his sleeping bag, hoping to catch a little sleep before the infrared detection alarms were triggered by another poxy rabbit. Or the roof fell in on him.

***

Back at base, Grabowski had shown his team satellite imagery indicating that the area surrounding the village was now a staging point for the next Russian offensive where troops and vehicles had been amassing in the area for weeks. Behind them, a wall of field guns and rocket launchers had been dug into position to provide cover for the advancing forces. A network of trenches and anti-tank traps surrounded them, where Russian Ground Forces had accepted the inevitable and were now planning for a long, drawn-out war of attrition. Using coloured markers, Grabowski had circled the hazards they needed to avoid, mercilessly drilling the men until they could recall each position, and the waypoints needed to navigate them, from memory.

"I can't help you with the unknowns though. We have virtually zero intel on minefields and monitoring stations, so you will need to keep your wits about you. Just because we don't know about them, doesn't mean they don't exist," Grabowski had warned.

Despite the complexity of the Russian defences, the first stage of Grabowski's plan was ridiculously simple - Wojciech and the team would just walk straight into the army camp around dawn. They would use the change of watch and usual early morning confusion as cover while they commandeered a vehicle for the drive north.

Having reached the river indicated by Grabowski, the Kapitan set a steady pace. They had around two hours to get to the Russian camp before dawn which should be plenty of time, assuming they didn't encounter any patrols or unidentified troop positions. The last thing he wanted was to walk into a firefight or another minefield, didn't want to draw attention this early in the mission. Didn't want to draw attention to his team *at all*.

The sky was just starting to turn pink when they finally spotted the camp. Wojciech called a halt, allowing the men a short rest. Adam scanned the perimeter while the rest of the team huddled down in the bushes along the river bank. Having caught his breath, Wojciech made a short call back to Mission Control using Tomasz's encrypted satphone. "We're across," he whispered, "Now entering Vergilevka camp."

"Acknowledged. Tracking beacons are working perfectly, you are good to go," Grabowski's voice echoed as the call bounced across space, "*Powodzenia* gentlemen."

Wojciech folded the satphone's aerial, ending the call, then motioned the men to move forward, carefully and quietly.

"Remember lads, Russian only from here on in though."

Wojciech took one last look back towards the comparative safety of Ukraine and the distant ruined towers of Kharkiv. Somewhere even further west there were families, friends, angry bosses and lovers waiting for their safe return. He sighed, then turning north, led the team into the heart of madness.

Chapter Twenty

Entry to the camp had been insanely easy. There had been no fence on this side facing the frontline, the battle-scarred earth simply gave way to hundreds of camouflaged tents pitched in rows. They walked straight in, weaving between a pair of sandbagged machine gun positions staffed by yawning, disinterested soldiers who didn't give them a second look after spotting their Russian Ground Forces uniforms.

The local brigade appeared to be made up of forced conscripts and jaded infantry drawn from the poorer, rougher regions at the extreme edges of the Russian Federation - Chechnya, Ingushetia, Dagestan and the like. No one seemed to give a toss about discipline or security, nor did they challenge the five men walking into the camp. They had strolled past the field hospital and on through the rows of mud splattered accommodation tents. Soldiers slouched in the doorways, all wearing the same disinterested, dazed look of men with nothing to look forward to except the next fateful offensive. Some played cards, others cleaned weapons, but no one looked as though they were ready to take on the Ukrainian army any time soon. Some eyed the skies as if expecting an imminent drone strike. Everyone looked hungry and mean.

"It's a Wagner Division," muttered Wojciech.

"A what?"

"These guys are led by professional mercenaries but most are not trained soldiers at all. They're criminals who have been released from prison to serve on the front line. If they can survive six months, the state gives them a full pardon and they go free."

"So they're cannon fodder," noted Adam drily.

"Not exactly. Turns out they are surprisingly effective even if they are expendable. But they are also mean bastards, accused of countless war crimes. These guys have no hope in prison, so they have nothing to lose on the battlefield. The Ukrainians have been quite successful at disrupting their supply chains too, so these guys are poorly equipped and underfed. That makes them very unpredictable and dangerous. So keep your eyes open and don't underestimate them."

After several minutes walking they could see the command post in the distance, surrounded by slow-moving personnel going to and fro between the tents. Apparently the officers were infected by the same hopeless ennui as their infantry, worn down by a war of attrition where positions are gained and lost repeatedly, often in the space of a few hours at the cost of dozens of lives.

"Pick a vehicle," Wojciech said to Ksiądz.

The driver pointed at a low, tank-tracked vehicle with fearsome-looking rear-mounted thermobaric missile launcher array away in the distance. Even obscured under camouflage netting, the polished tubes holding the rockets shone brightly in the early morning light.

"That TOS-1 looks *perfect*," Ksiądz said grinning.

"OK, smart guy. And your second choice?"

"The Ural next to it," he shifted attention to a four-wheeled light cargo truck standing alongside the missile launcher, "It's nothing special, but it is reliable, perfect for what we want. It's also a little closer so we don't have to walk as far." Nothing special was right. The truck looked battered and bruised, even more beaten and decrepit than the soldiers they had just passed.

The team arrived at the Ural unchallenged and Paweł, Tomasz and Adam hauled themselves up into the canvas-covered rear section. Ksiądz paused to sprinkle some holy water on the truck, then climbed into the driver's seat. He was mildly disappointed to find the keys waiting for him in the ignition. The engine was already running by the time Wojciech settled into the passenger seat. Ksiądz carefully hung his rosary over the central console, released the handbrake, ground his way through the gears and eased the truck onto the muddy, rutted track that would take them off the base.

A fence had been built around the tent city, but the effort was woeful - just two lazy rows of barbed wire that snaked in both directions. "I guess it makes sense really," said Ksiądz, "who wants to break into a Russian forward camp anyway?"

"Especially one full of violent criminals," added Adam.

"Us?" Tomasz was in a particularly sarcastic mood.

Ksiądz nosed the Ural gently towards a gap in the wire where two privates stood outside a tin shack, guarding the entrance to the camp. Ksiądz slowed the truck as if to stop, but the soldiers simply waved him on.

"It doesn't look like the Army is as committed to this war as their Supreme Commander in Chief," noted Wojciech drily as they pulled on to a made road and headed north towards Belgorod, "Now let's put some kilometres in before someone notices this truck is missing."

Chapter Twenty-One

"We need to dump this vehicle soon," warned Ksiądz, "One army truck, travelling away from the front, alone. Eventually we're going to attract attention."

"I definitely don't want to be caught and shot as a deserter from an army I don't even serve," laughed Adam grimly.

"Keep a lookout for somewhere suitable then," said Wojciech, as they sped north on the M2 highway towards Belgorod, "Preferably before we reach the city."

The sun was high in the sky and the roads were busy, life apparently quite normal on this side of the front line.

"There," Ksiądz pointed to a small roadside café up ahead, a low, battered building. The tin roof looked rusted through in places and a few flakes of green paint clung determinedly to the wooden walls. It looked more like a place of last resort than somewhere to stop for a good meal. He pulled the truck into the gravelled carpark and continued past the building, following a rough farm track into some trees opposite. After bouncing violently for a hundred metres or so, he steered the Ural further into the woods, and turned off the engine. The team got to work spreading netting across the abandoned vehicle, then covering them with branches and leaves. It was far from perfect, but it would be good enough to buy them some time while they continued north.

They walked back up the track towards the café, careful to stay out of view of the road. Ksiądz handed his rucksack and rifle to Tomasz and jogged ahead. Paweł trained his pistol on the door to the café just in case they were interrupted. There were a handful of cars and a battered green UAZ van parked outside the building, ideal for what they needed. Grabbing a screwdriver, he set to work on an ancient Lada, prying off the registration plates. He swapped them with the UAZ, a task that took just two minutes. He paused for a moment to fish a hip flask from his pocket, splashing a few drops of liquid onto the van, "May God bless and protect this vehicle and all who travel in her."

Dedication complete, he forced his screwdriver into the van's lock, smiling as it popped open with barely any effort. Sat in the driver's seat, he repeated the manoeuvre on the ignition barrel, laughing as the engine choked and coughed into life. He removed his rosary and wrapped it carefully around the rear view mirror.

The rest of the team climbed into the truck and he pulled back onto the highway. Adam scoured the road behind for any sign that they had been spotted, or that the police were following, but it seemed to be clear for now.

"Are you still blessing every vehicle you drive?" Paweł asked.

"Only the ones I steal," Ksiądz grinned.

"You didn't complain in Kandahar," Wojciech added.

After another few kilometres, Ksiądz stopped at another roadside café to perform a second plate swap, "That should make it much harder to follow us. Just remind me we'll need to do it a few times as we travel between registration regions."

Apparently the van belonged to a builder - the back was filled with tools, planks of wood, assorted garbage and a thick layer of brick dust and cement. Wojciech sat in the passenger seat alongside Ksiądz while the rest of the team spread out on the floor, trying to get some rest. Even with most of the builder's junk pushed to one side of the van, the stiff suspension and potholed road surface made for an uncomfortable ride.

"Only another 1200 kilometres to go, my friends," Ksiądz yelled above the noise of the engine, "Are we having fun yet?"

"We will be if Adam keeps his stinking feet away from my face," Tomasz growled.

Chapter Twenty-Two

Nestled just inside the Kremlin walls in central Moscow, Block 14 looks like any other imperial Russian building. A striking mustard-coloured imperial Russian building that is. Block 14 is home to the Federal Protective Service, the government agency responsible for providing security for Russian state officials. Despite being less well-known than its post-KGB sibling the FSB, the FSO boasts the same levels of autonomy and power - including control of Russia's nuclear launch codes.

General Dmitry Chernov, a bulky, barrel-chested man, was conducting his daily briefing with the FSO heads of department to discuss their most recent findings. He sat at the head of a long wooden table, flanked by senior officers and department heads, listening to their mundane reports and observations.

Today was slightly different however, in that he was being addressed by Yuri Ovechkin, a middle ranking FSO officer, usually considered too low-level to be anywhere near the conference room. But he had insisted he had urgent intel of national significance. Normally Chernov would have ignored the man's pleas, but he felt sorry for him, recognised the same hunger that he had before achieving his ambitions. So he had indulged the man, allowing him to attend the briefing and present his intelligence report at the end of the meeting.

Ovechkin wasn't young however, and he would not be advancing any further up the greasy pole of the FSO. He was middle-aged, grey-haired and well into the latter stages of an unremarkable career. Less intelligence agent, more university professor thought Chernov. One that had been sleeping on the streets for a fortnight, often forgetting to wash, shave or change his clothes. Looking at the state of the man, Chernov wondered if he had made a mistake allowing him into the meeting.

"We have had reports that Poland has successfully tracked the President's movements and is encouraging the US or the British to make a move on him," Ovechkin was saying.

"Yes, yes, we already know this Yuri," Chernov nodded, "But we have also heard from our NATO sources that the Americans have refused. The Americans and everyone else for that matter."

"Perhaps," the man said, tilting his head on one side, "But now we are hearing from a Ukrainian source near Kharkiv that the Poles may try something themselves."

"And risk dragging NATO into our special military operation? Turn it into an actual war?" Chernov chuckled, "No, I really don't think they will."

"Normally I would agree General," the man said, head still tilted for no reason that Chernov could fathom, "But last night we received a report of a small team crossing the border into Russia, just north of Kharkiv."

"Again, this is nothing new Yuri" the General

sighed, "The Ukrainians are always sending spies across the frontline on reconnaissance missions, just as we do. We look at their positions, they look at ours. It's called *war*."

The other men sat around the table snickered.

"They tend to avoid our basecamps though, sir," his head suddenly flipped back to its upright position, "We believe these men marched into the middle of a Wagner division before stealing a vehicle."

"Kharkiv you say?" Chernov stared at the peeling ceiling for a moment, "And you think they are going to what? Drive all the way to the Kremlin, past our entire army and assassinate President Leontin in his office?"

This time the other men in the briefing laughed at the ridiculousness of the scenario.

"I think it most likely that some of those Wagner dogs have stolen the vehicle themselves and are trying to escape their patriotic duty," the General said, "But you can assign a small team to investigate if you need to Yuri."

"Thank you General," the man nodded, clearly relieved.

"A *small* team Yuri. You and Pushkin. In the unlikely event that you discover anything, your are to inform me immediately. And Sokolov. The SPB needs to know if there is a credible threat too," said Chernov standing up, "Now unless there is anything else, I have another meeting…"

Chairs scraped back from the table and Ovechkin hurried back to his own office. "Chernov gave us the go ahead," he said to the young man sat opposite, "Call Belgorod and get someone to trace that missing vehicle. Now."

Chapter Twenty-Three

The discomfort of the van and the heady scent of dried sweat and stale adrenaline seemed to make the journey even slower. That and the rancid stench rising from Adam's toes. Alpha Team successfully skirted Belgorod but had to stop for fuel shortly afterwards. The men took the opportunity to change out of their stolen Russian uniforms and into some casual clothes. Wojciech even produced a pack of wet wipes from somewhere, so each man could give his armpits a quick scrub. "Parental habits die hard," he said with a shrug.

"Leontin will never smell us coming," grinned Tomasz, "except maybe Adam's feet of course."

"Just keep your weapons out of sight," cautioned Paweł, "And whatever you do, don't let anyone see inside Gennady's pack."

"What *did* he give you Paweł?" Adam asked.

"We'll divide it all up when we get closer to the target, but there's a few extras that may come in handy," he smiled.

While Wojciech had been pumping fuel, Ksiądz had been busy switching registration plates again. Then they were back on the road, this time apparently driving a van from the Kursk oblast.

"Check-in time Tomasz," Wojciech called out, "Give Warsaw a status update."

Tomasz produced the encrypted sat phone, extended the folding antenna and punched the speed dial button that would connect him to the Warsaw control room.

Grabowski answered on the first ring, "You're making good time. We saw you change vehicles, any problems?"

"All clear sir. Are the trackers still working?" Tomasz queried.

"Signals are loud and clear. Check in again when you reach Oryol."

"Very good sir," said Tomasz, cutting the call.

"Get some sleep Paweł and Adam," instructed Wojciech, "You'll be driving once we reach Kursk."

The two men stretched out on the floor of the van, as instructed.

"Ksiądz, I have another question for you" said Tomasz mischievously, "The Ukrainians say they have God on their side, as do the Russians. Both say they are fighting a holy war. So whose side is God really on?"

Ksiądz rolled his eyes, "He's on everyone's side Tomasz. He's interested in souls, not territory or politics. He wants Zelenskyy *and* Leontin and all the other poor bastards out there on the battlefield. He even wants you. After all, every soldier becomes a believer when they're on the frontline."

"Would you two theologians shut up and let us get some rest?" Paweł yelled from the back of the van.

"Yes sir," Ksiądz laughed.

***

Wojciech woke with a start. He hadn't meant to fall asleep, but it had been a long night. It took him a moment to realise what had woken him - the van had stopped and he could hear voices. Tomasz and Ksiądz were speaking to someone outside the driver's window.

"I'm sorry officer, but I definitely wasn't speeding."

Wojciech could see a traffic cop craning to peer around Ksiądz, "Yes sir, you were. And now I see you have passengers in the back? Without seatbelts? This is very bad. Very bad indeed. Your papers, now please."

Leytenant politsii Novikov knew he had taken a risk pulling the van over, but he was hoping to find a relatively well paid tradesman onboard. Instead he had ended up apprehending a crew of surly, burly looking men with strange accents. It looked like these weirdos were sleeping in the van. But it is what it is - and he needed to make something from this stop.

Tomasz tugged at his shirt pocket so the cop could see a 5000 rubles note tucked inside, "Can we make a deal?"

5000 rubles, is this guy for real? Novikov stared in outraged disbelief, eyeballs bulging in anger. "You, out of the van. Now. And you," he pointed at Ksiądz, "open the hood."

Ducking sideways out of view, Wojciech unholstered his pistol, heart pounding as the adrenaline began racing. Tomasz saw the movement and gave a barely perceptible shake of the head. "*Da* officer," he said, raising his hands placatingly, then stepping out into the road and walked around the front of the van as instructed. Ksiądz popped the release catch, and the traffic cop lifted the hood, leaving the team unable to see what was going on.

"What is happening?" Wojciech whispered to Ksiądz.

"I don't know *kapitan*. I can hear voices but I cannot make out what they are saying."

Outside, Tomasz was trying to placate the officer. "I am sorry sir. I did not mean to offend."

Novikov had begun to calm, his well-practiced routine going the way it always did. "Obviously this is a very serious matter. I could take your license and have you summoned to traffic court. Speeding. Three passengers travelling without seatbelts. And that's before I even check you have the correct paperwork and forms. That's a lot of charges you are facing - and the fines will be quite severe."

"Yes, I see that," said Tomasz nodding, "What can I do for you?"

The cop sighed and leaned over the engine, pretending to examine the battery. There was something odd about this group of men, but he couldn't put his finger on it. The uncertainty annoyed him because he was sure he could extract a larger bribe if he could just figure out what their secret was. Perhaps they were transporting drugs?

Tomasz dug into his pocket and produced a two more 5000 rubles banknotes. He leaned forward into the engine compartment, hands braced against the bodywork and slid the reddish notes towards the officer. Novikov glanced at the cash, *that's more like it*.

"I think we can help each other after all," said the cop, pulling the money gently from under Tomasz's hand, "Perhaps I was mistaken about your speed. Please take care."

Novikov stood up, stuffed the two notes into his trouser and straightened his cap. He glanced once more into the van and its occupants before sauntering back to his patrol car. *Not a bad result,* he thought, smiling to himself as climbed into the driver's seat, *5000 rubles for him, 5000 rubles for his wife and an extra 5000 rubles with which to treat his mistress. Much better than expected.* He drove slowly past the UAZ, eyeballing Tomasz as he went. *A pleasure doing business with you!*

When the patrol car finally disappeared out of sight, Tomasz dropped the bonnet and climbed back into the van. Sat in the rear, Wojciech returned his pistol to its holster and wiped the sweat from his brow. It had been a very close call and shooting a cop would have triggered a manhunt - not to mention a moral crisis at killing an innocent.

"I swear I wasn't speeding," Ksiądz was pleading.

"No, you weren't, this was just a routine encounter with local Russian bureaucracy," agreed Tomasz, "And an expensive one at that, he just cost us nearly 675 złoty. I'll put it on Grabowski's tab."

Ksiądz laughed nervously, but his smile did not reach his eyes, "Let's just hope he doesn't get curious and run the plates."

There was a loud snore from the far end of the van. Adam had slept through the entire encounter.

"How does he do that?" asked Paweł jealously.

Chapter Twenty-Four

"We found the Ural, sir," the Belgorod agent was saying, "It was dumped in some woodland off the M2, south of the city, just like you said it would be."

"So what vehicle are they in now?" Ovechkin was excited about the chase and worried about what it may mean.

"There is a roadside café near here. A green UAZ van belonging to a local builder was stolen from the car park out front. The owner is raging, all of his tools were in the back of the vehicle."

"And do you have the registration plates?"

"I thought that we needed to act quickly, so I have already circulated the details to the local police. We will have them soon," said the Belgorod man with a trace of pride in his voice.

"Did you check the other cars first?"

"Uh, for what sir?" he didn't sound so confident now.

"For the missing plates," Ovechkin said, his impatience rising, "Did you check the plates of the other cars at the café?"

He could hear the cogs grinding in his agent's brain, "Oh sh…"

The line went dead. A few moments later Ovechkin's phone rang again.

"I'm sorry sir, they *did* switch plates. Apparently the UAZ van is driving on plates belonging to an ancient Lada Niva."

"Circulate the updated details then," said Ovechkin, "Unfortunately I suspect that these men are already a step ahead of us and will have switched plates again. Ask the police to report *any* car or registration plate thefts in your oblast."

He paused and tapped his knuckles on his desk for a moment. Obviously the intel from the frontline observation post was good and a foreign team was active inside Russia. The whispers coming out of Poland confirmed it. And he was not dealing with amateurs either. But what was this team were doing? Whatever it was, the FSO needed to get ahead of them before they could complete their mission or disappear.

"On second thoughts, circulate the same request to police in all the neighbouring oblasts between Belgorod and Moscow. These men are doing more than just scouting the front line or our supply routes. Oh, and let the builder know that he will probably have his UAZ and tools back unharmed before the end of the day."

He hung up the phone, the drumming of his knuckles becoming faster and more insistent. If these men wanted to get to Moscow, there had to be easier ways to do it. A bus from Belarus or a flight from Turkey should be simple enough with the right forged paperwork. Unless they were acting alone? There was no way a rogue unit would pull a stunt like this? But mercenaries wouldn't breach Russian borders for any amount of money… What the hell was going on?

***

The call about the UAZ had come over the radio while police lieutenant Novikov sat watching traffic flow along the M2. He remembered the group of men with the strange accents he could not identify crammed into the battered green builder's van. He also remembered the 15,000 rubles he had taken from them. Accepting bribes was perfectly commonplace, almost expected in his job, and he knew his captain would not care. The old bastard would probably congratulate him for such a big score.

But this emergency call sounded different, something more significant than the usual escaping robbers or gangsters. Like there were higher-ups involved. Different enough that he was going to deny ever having seen the UAZ and its occupants. He started the patrol car and drove to his mistress' house instead.

Chapter Twenty-Five

"The Wagner division at Vergilevka were extremely unhelpful," the Belgorod FSO agent was saying, "They did not want to talk at all. Seems they expect the theft to be added onto their prison sentences."

"That's assuming they survive their six month tour of duty," Ovechkin growled into his phone.

"The local commander checked and it seems that there's a canvas-covered Ural missing, but no one actually saw who took it. The guards on the gate remember it passing, but they didn't bother to check who was onboard. We do know that all the men on base are accounted for though. Clearly the truck was taken by a third party."

Ovechkin tapped a few keys to call up a map of the area surrounding the base on his computer. Whoever it was had chosen to cross the border in that area for a reason. And the only reason he could see was easy access to the M2 highway. It's not as though Belgorod was famous for its food or cultural sights even before the war.

"They won't have kept the Ural for long," he said, thinking aloud, "I want you to find it. They will have dumped the truck somewhere on the M2, *before* Belgorod where it would have drawn too much attention. They will have switched to another vehicle. Check shopping malls, offices, restaurants. Anywhere along the highway where there are plenty of cars to be stolen."

"Very good," replied the Belgorod agent, "I will call again when I have an update."

"Perhaps we should let some of the Wagner animals loose after them?" Pushkin suggested.

"Don't tempt me," his boss replied.

***

Paweł had taken the wheel at Kursk, nearly two hours earlier. Tomasz and Ksiądz were asleep in the back, while Wojciech had given up the passenger seat to Adam. He leaned through the gap and took the GPS off the UAZ's dashboard.

"Changing plates is useful, but if we are travelling on the highways, I think we need to change vehicles again too." He swiped around the satellite image map, eventually finding what he was looking for. "Here, on the outskirts of Oryol. There's a big factory with a large car park. We'll find something there."

Fifteen minutes later, Paweł pulled across the highway and into an industrial estate, surrounded by dozens of cars. Wojciech pointed to a smaller overflow car park off to the left, behind some empty storage containers. Moments later the battered UAZ had been swapped for a white Patriot SUV. A few seconds more and the registration plates had been exchanged with another nearby car. After a quick baptism (Ksiądz insisted) the SUV was pulling across the M2, travelling north, rosary swinging wildly from the rear view mirror as the vehicle accelerated.

"We've probably got a few hours until the next shift change at that factory," said Ksiądz, but if anyone sees another Patriot on the way, let me know and we'll do the plates again."

"Speaking of registration plates, follow the signs for the P92," instructed Wojciech, "We can't afford to get caught on a toll road driving a car with mismatched tags."

The SUV was smaller than the UAZ, and the three men in the back grumbled about the lack of personal space, elbowing each other to emphasise the point. But the Patriot was also newer and faster, so they were quickly through the city and out the other side, travelling north towards Kaluga. The road seemed to wind endlessly between sun drenched fields filled with various crops, all caught in that period of limbo between the first sprouts of spring and end of summer harvest, green everywhere. It would still be some weeks until the fields would be full of farmers and labourers, taking in their produce and preparing it for sale or storage. For now it was just a riot of green, flashing by on both sides of the highway. Periodically they would pass through a village, followed by winding bends that were already treacherous because of the poorly maintained road. The cement surface was scarred with potholes, and every time they hit one the passengers were thrown into the air while Adam cursed loudly from behind the wheel.

"I can't wait until it's someone else's turn to drive," he muttered through clenched teeth.

"I assure you it's even worse trying to sleep back here," Wojciech called back groggily before kicking the back of Adam's seat to show his displeasure.

Chapter Twenty-Six

An hour later, the Belgorod agent was back on the phone with another report.

"They ditched the UAZ and we think they may have switched into a white Patriot SUV," he said breathlessly.

"Where?" demanded Ovechkin.

"A factory outside Oryol sir."

"When?"

"Two hours ago sir."

Ovechkin traced the route on his map; the men were still headed straight up the highway in the direction of Moscow. They were at least two hours out, but no doubt making good time now they were in a more capable vehicle.

"Contact the Moscow police," he said, "have them put checkpoints on the A113 and AH8, AH6 and E115 ring roads. Tell them to stop any vehicle carrying five or more men."

"But sir, the disruption…" the Belgorod man began to complain.

"Under my authority. Any questions or reports are to come to me direct. My team will take over from here. Thank you."

Ovechkin replaced the phone, deep in thought,

drumming his fingers gently on the map. Two sets of roadblocks between Oryol and Moscow *should* be enough to pick these men up - or to at least deter them from entering the capital. And yet, something still didn't add up - and he couldn't put his finger on what he was missing.

***

The decision to avoid Moscow was an easy one. Wojciech had no reason to think the Russians even knew they existed, but it seemed wise to limit the number of people who might see them. There were any number of innocent reasons why a group of men may be travelling together, but why risk encountering an over-zealous traffic cop? And that was before considering the numerous toll roads that made up the Moscow ring road, each one an opportunity to be caught in a stolen vehicle with dodgy plates. Going cross-country would take longer, but it was also much safer because there would be fewer chances to encounter police or security services.

At Kaluga, Tomasz took the wheel, steering the SUV north through the Moscow Uplands. Cultivated fields gave way to extended spaces of scrubland dotted with the occasional wood. The road wound over small hills and through shallow valleys, the undulating countryside interspersed with small villages and larger cities where daily life seemed to continue undisturbed. *It's hard to believe we're on the brink of a nuclear war*, Wojciech thought as he watched the greenery rolling by.

"Hey, Adam," Paweł called out, "what happened to that girl you seeing? The one with the weird eye? What was her name Ewa? Ewelina? She was nuts."

"Edyta. I married her," the sniper replied drily.

"Oh," Paweł could feel his foot lodged firmly in the back of his throat, "Congratulations!"

The other men snickered nervously.

"Yes. We also have a son with a weird eye together."

"*Gratulacja* again!" Paweł wished the ground would open up and swallow him, "Listen, I didn't mean to be rude when I said…"

"Sorry brother," Adam was roaring with laughter, "Edyta broke up with me not long after we got back from Kandahar. Said she was done with country living and hunting, never wanted to eat venison again. Had a problem with my beard too."

"And your comrades constantly taking the piss out of her eye," Tomasz added.

"Last I heard she had moved to Warsaw, married a clean-shaven architect and become a vegetarian," Adam added with a grin.

Wojciech slapped his weapons specialist on the shoulder, "He *really* got you."

Their laughter was long and hard.

***

It had been two hours but still there was no reports of a Patriot carrying a group of men. They had simply vanished into thin air. Either the team had found an alternative way into Moscow, or someone had screwed up on the checkpoints. Ovechkin knew it was the checkpoints. It was always the checkpoints manned by corrupt or stupid provincial cops. He ran his hands through his wild hair and stared at the phone, willing it to ring.

Chapter Twenty-Seven

They had been making good time when they pulled into the city of Uvarovka to refuel. Yet another semi-derelict service station on the outskirts of another grey concrete urban sprawl. Four rusting pumps thrust through the cracked cement floor under a bent and misshapen iron roof - and the watchful eye of a mean-looking, heavily tattooed attendant.

Ksiądz pumped diesel while the other men stretched their legs. He walked over and paid the cashier, using the opportunity to scan the lot for a new vehicle. Seeing nothing suitable, the Priest and Wojciech climbed reluctantly back into the car. Tomasz followed them, but his boot slipped on the running board. Struggling to regain his balance he grabbed at something, anything, to stop him falling. His flailing hand caught at the weapons holdall under the seat, pulling it out of the SUV as he landed on his backside. There was a loud clatter and an AK-12 spilled out onto the cement just as a police patrol car pulled onto the petrol station forecourt behind them.

Tomasz scooped up the rifle and threw it into the car before diving in himself. "Go, go, go!" He yelled and Ksiądz accelerated quickly away. Their car bounced over the kerb and lurched violently as the Priest wrestled the steering wheel to the left.

"Did the cop see us?" Asked Wojciech.

Ksiądz glanced in the rear view mirror to see the police car quickly gaining ground, blue lights blazing, "Yes. Yes he did."

He continued to accelerate and they were soon in the outskirts of the city. As the houses and apartment blocks thinned, the trees thickened, forest sloping away on both sides of the road. The police car was easily keeping pace with the heavy-laden SUV - and others were certain to join the chase very soon.

"Adam, I need you to put him off the road, and out of sight," said Wojciech, "Quickly."

Adam pointed his sniper rifle towards the rear windscreen, resting the barrel on the back of the seats. "Cover your ears," he said.

There was an enormous bang and the air inside the SUV was sucked out as the rear window exploded in a spray of glass. The last thing Adam saw before the windscreen of the police car erupted was the face of the police officer behind the wheel, twisted in a grimace of terror. Then the car jerked violently to the right, becoming airborne before cartwheeling away into the trees by the roadside.

Wojciech could barely hear the rushing wind whirling in through the broken window over the sound of ringing in his ears. "Did you kill him?" He asked Adam.

Adam pointed at his own ears and shrugged, *I hope not*, he mouthed. Ksiądz crossed himself, mouthing a silent prayer.

"We need to find another vehicle as quickly as possible," the Priest yelled from the front seat.

***

Ovechkin was staring at the map again when the phone rang.

"I have received a strange report sir," said a young man's voice, "It may not be anything at all to do with the men you're looking for, but you did say to call if anything unusual came in…"

"And…?"

"We've heard from the municipal police station in Uvarovka. Apparently one of their traffic officers radioed in about some armed men at a petrol station in the city."

"And…?" Ovechkin located Uvarovka on his map.

"He said he was going to stop the vehicle because he suspected it was being used by an OPG. A white Patriot. But he hasn't been heard from since."

"When was this?"

"About an hour ago."

"Keep me updated," Ovechkin said, replacing the handset absentmindedly. His mind was already onto the next stage of the chase as he traced the route between Kaluga and Uvarovka. The policeman could be have stumbled onto an organised crime group, but what business would they have in a nowhere town like Uvarovka? No, this had to be the men he was pursuing. A sloppy mistake giving him his first stroke of luck.

Clearly the team was not headed for Moscow. In fact, they seemed to be going out of their way to avoid the capital, travelling west then north. He drummed his knuckles on the table, a relentless, driving rhythm that resonated with something deep inside his own nervous energy.

They were just one hour behind their prey - but only if they could figure out where the men were going - and what vehicle they would switch into next. Now they had been spotted, they would dump the Patriot as quickly as possible. He stared at the map, willing it to reveal a destination, but the roads and contours held their peace.

If they made it as far as the intersection at Shakhovskaya they could run east for safety the Latvian border - *if* they could get through the fence. But why would they enter Russian territory just to steal some cars before leaving again? A basic scouting mission seems unlikely given that almost everything in that region is visible by satellite anyway. Troop movements, gun emplacements and convoys could all be clearly seen from space, as the Ukrainians had shown with their increasingly accurate drone attacks. If the men headed west the road would take them back into Moscow, a place they had clearly been avoiding. South would mean retracing their steps, straight into the arms of the police who they knew are following after the incident at the service station. Again, pointless. That left north, and a straight run to Tver, but for what reason?

He checked his watch, realising the men had almost certainly passed Shakhovskaya, so they would have already chosen a direction and taken it. Now he knew they were serious, Ovechkin briefly considered reporting the incursion to General Chernov so that he could request more resources for the manhunt. Then remembering the way in which the General had scorned him in front of the department heads, *Screw him, we'll do it ourselves.* He sighed, rubbed his dry, scratchy eyes and began calling local police asking them to watch for five or six men travelling on the M9 highway or the regional road travelling towards Tver.

Chapter Twenty-Eight

Now that the operation hung by a thread, tension in the team was higher than ever. They pulled into a second hand car lot, dumping the Patriot amongst the other vehicles. Pushing down hard on his guilt for the police officer, Ksiądz set about breaking into two sedans, and starting their engines. Stepping back, he instinctively reached into his pocket and retrieved his flask of holy water.

"Ksiądz, we don't have time for that," Paweł hissed, hopping from foot to foot impatiently.

"We don't have time *not* to do it," Wojciech hissed back.

Splitting the team into two vehicles was far from ideal, but the police would definitely be looking for five men travelling together now. Wojciech was confident that if they could get past Tver, they would escape whatever trap the Russian had set. And he had no doubt that there would be a trap waiting for them where the roads converged.

Wojciech, Ksiądz and Tomasz would be in the lead vehicle, an ugly burnt orange Lada Kalina station wagon. "Look at all that boot space," Ksiądz said, mimicking a used car salesman, "Plenty of room for all the kids' stuff. Or military hardware." He tossed his pack into the boot.

Paweł and Adam would follow a discreet distance

behind in a metallic brown Lada Vesta sedan. "Brown because it's shit," Paweł muttered.

The men huddled around the Kalina while Wojciech delivered a hurried briefing, "If we are separated for any reason, we'll meet at the filling station at S Yedrovo on the M10 at 0200." He showed Paweł the rendezvous point on his GPS and made sure the weapons expert programmed the correct location into his own device. "If either car fails to turn up, the mission is aborted and you're to make your way to the nearest border as quickly as possible. Questions?"

"Will you be buying breakfast?" Asked Tomasz, grinning widely.

Satisfied they knew what they were doing, Wojciech tapped the bonnet and the men moved away to their assigned cars. Despite Paweł's concerns, the whole changeover took less than ten minutes, including Ksiądz's baptismal ritual.

***

Ovechkin had waited an hour but none of the patrols had reported anything. A call had come in from Uvarovka to say they had found their missing police officer. He was badly injured but alive, trapped behind the wheel of his crumpled patrol car somewhere just off the highway, apparently downed by a single, large caliber round. But the men he was chasing seemed to have vanished. He jabbed his finger at the map - it had to be Tver.

"I need roadblocks on the Lebedevo highway," he yelled into the phone, "I want you to check every car coming into Tver or joining the M11 highway."

"But sir," spluttered the Tver chief of police,

"Surely not every one?"

"Yes!" Ovechkin yelled,"Every. Single. One." He slammed his handset down before the man could argue further.

"Pushkin!" He shouted at his deputy, "Get us a helicopter. We're going to Tver. Now!"

***

Tomasz terminated the call, "The electronic surveillance team is picking up a lot of chatter on the police networks about a manhunt for a team of foreign spies. They know about the police car and the Patriot and they nearly had us back at Shakhovskaya. Now they are assembling roadblocks at Tver."

Wojciech took a moment, staring out the window as the darkening countryside rushed by. He could imagine communications networks across western Russia lighting up as word of the foreign infiltrators spread like a fire. Every cop, soldier, agent and informant this side of Moscow would be on the look-out for them now. "We're going to have to go cross country," he said, fingers swiping hurriedly on the screen of his GPS.

Immediately he could see there was a problem. No matter which northerly route they took, unless they got to one of the bridges at Tver there was no way across the mighty Volga river. He dragged the map south in the opposite direction. There was another road with an alternative crossing if they turned back on themselves, but the detour that would add hundreds of kilometres and several hours to their journey time. He checked his watch and shook his head, not an option; rerouting would take too long, they would miss their deadline. Instead they would have to stay the course, take their chances and find out whether they really were on a mission from God or not.

"Paweł, take the road signposted D Polubratavo and follow it though to the next highway," Wojciech said over the radio, "And keep it subtle. We're going through smaller towns where the locals probably will notice strange vehicles late at night."

"*Tak, kapitan.*"

Chapter Twenty-Nine

The helicopter flight to Migalovo took less than two hours because the pilot had thrashed the Mi-8 as hard as possible; he wanted rid of his FSO cargo. Especially since the call had come in from the Kremlin. Chernov was frothing with rage, "You blocked the southern entrances to Moscow and now you're doing the same in Tver? What the hell are you playing at Ovechkin?"

"We have reason to believe there is a team of foreign agents operating on Russian soil sir," the FSO man's voice betrayed a quiet confidence, "They slipped through in Moscow but we will catch them at Tver."

"I said no disruptions Ovechkin, no trouble, no nonsense. Instead you bring half the country to a halt chasing an imaginary team of spies. Those roadblocks are to be removed immediately - and then I want you back here in my office."

"Very good sir," Ovechkin replied. He sat back in his seat and stared angrily through the plexiglass window to his left.

"Do you want me to call the chief of police in Tver, sir?" Pushkin asked.

"Absolutely not," Ovechkin said, shaking his head.

"But…"

"But nothing," the senior man snapped, "We're going to see this through, with or without Chernov's blessing. That short-sighted, pig-ignorant bastard will thank me when we catch these intruders."

Pushkin sank back in his seat. His career in the FSO was over, incinerated by his delusional boss. How would he explain this to his wife?

The bulbous aircraft had come low over the M11, allowing Ovechkin to observe the chaos caused by his roadblocks, queues of cars stretching far off into the darkness below like a chain of pathetic Christmas lights. He smiled weakly, imagining Chernov's phone ringing red hot with complaints back in Moscow.

Within moments they were gliding above another smaller road to clear the fence and land in the Migalovo Air Base where a car was waiting to take him Ovechkin and Pushkin to the operational command post. Ovechkin glowered at a steady stream of fast moving cars passing just a few feet below the wheels of the helicopter and slapped his forehead.

Where were all these cars coming from? And why was no one checking them as they joined the highway?

***

Ksiądz gasped as a fat, ugly helicopter passed directly overhead, landing in a large fenced-off compound to the left of the highway. The clattering rotors shook the poorly constructed car, the sound reverberating inside his skull. He was sure he could even see the faces of the people onboard peering through the round porthole windows, one of them slapping his forehead angrily as he stared at the cars below.

"Odd," he muttered, following the arcing slip road

onto the westbound M10 highway and picking up speed once more, the lights of Tver quickly receding in his mirrors.

***

After witnessing the checkpoint debacle first hand, Ovechkin had given orders for the checkpoint operation to be dismantled as quickly as possible. Then he had one of the officers drive him and Pushkin to the Tver central police station. Without waiting for an invitation, he stormed into the chief's office and began voicing his displeasure. Loudly. The local man cowered as the senior FSO agent leaned over his desk, yelling obscenities. Pushkin stood by the door, squirming with embarrassment and wishing that he could just melt away into the ground.

"But sir," the Chief tried to defend himself, "we carried out your orders to the letter. We checked every car joining the M11 from Shakhoyskaya."

"And you didn't think to check the other northbound roads?" Overchkin spat back.

"We used our limited resources to carry out your order, sir," the chief shrugged apologetically, "and we still have no idea what you are actually looking for. Who are these men? What are they so important?"

Ovechkin paused, he still didn't know why this team of five unknown men mattered. But he wasn't going to let a provincial policeman better him, "That's FSO business. You just do what you're told. *Kapitan*." He slammed his fist on the desk hard enough to knock a pile of papers onto the floor, turned on his heel and slammed the Chief's door, hard. Pushkin smiled a weak apology to the Chief and then let himself out of the office as quietly as possible.

***

Sat in the back of another squad car on the way back to Migalovo Air Base, Ovechkin made a call to Alexey Sokolov in Block 14 of the Kremlin. "Alexey, my friend. It has been a while. How is your family?" his tone was oily, hoping to charm the man on the other end of the phone.

"Yuri," the man said with a sigh, "I am extremely busy today and I have no time for pleasantries. What is it that you want?"

"Alexey, is there something unusual happening in your department today? Something big?"

"You know that I cannot tell you this Yuri. I cannot discuss SPB business with you."

The President Security Service, SPB for short, is a small sub-directorate of Yuri's own FSO, charged with protecting the safety of the Russian president. And although they worked in the same building, the SPB was forbidden from sharing information with the FSO to prevent leaks that could place the President in danger.

"Alexey, you know that I would never ask unless it was important. Unless the life of the President himself was in danger."

"If that were the case Yuri, then you would have done your duty and reported your intel to the SPB."

"Alexey, I have no time to waste on petty departmental squabbles. So just tell me, is the President leaving Moscow tomorrow?"

"He may be."

"Will he be heading north west?"

"He may be."

"But stopping short of St Petersburg?"

"Enough Yuri," the SPB man sighed, "This is much, much bigger than you realise. What is going on?"

Ovechkin cut the call. "I know where they are going," he said to Pushkin smiling, "We can still catch them."

***

Back in Moscow, Sokolov stared at the phone. What game was Ovechkin playing? And did it have something to do with the old spy in Poland? He replayed the call in his mind but could not see any immediate threats or connections.

In a way he felt sorry for the dead agents in Warsaw, so desperate to find some meaning in their old age, like Ovechkin. Sokolov not seen much of the Cold War himself but he had definitely seen what it did to the minds of his commanding officers, how many of them still lived in the past where an American CIA agent was hiding in every shadow. And since Ukraine, he had started to see the same thought patterns in his Kremlin colleagues.

He shook his head and turned his attention to finalising some travel and security plans for the President and a 'high profile guest'.

He shuffled papers for a few moments and then stopped. Where *was* Ovechkin?

Chapter Thirty

The S Yedrovo petrol station was nearly deserted, just a few long distance trucks parked at the edges of the forecourt, away from the petrol pumps and their flickering fluorescent lights so the drivers could sleep. The Kalina arrived first, doing a slow lap of the car park before pulling up at one of the pumps. A few minutes later the Vesta pulled alongside. The men unfolded themselves from the cars taking the opportunity to stretch their aching limbs, careful to stay in the shadows and away from the CCTV cameras mounted in the roof canopy above the fuel pumps.

There would be fewer potential witnesses at this hour of the night, thought Wojciech, but that may make us more memorable to the cashier working the graveyard shift - especially after buying five plastic-looking sandwiches and a six-pack of Coke. Thankfully the team was nearing their final destination and it wouldn't matter after that.

"Let's move out," he called to his men, "We'll find somewhere to rest for a few hours."

***

Sokolov had sent word that Ovechkin was to call him immediately but the call never came. He had sat at his desk and smoked silently for a few hours before eventually nodding off to sleep in his chair. The shrill ring of the phone made him jump and he snatched up the receiver, "Ovechkin, where the hell…?"

"No, Alexey, it is me, Vladimir."

"I am sorry, Vladimir Vladimirovich. How can I help you? It is rather late…"

The President interrupted him again, "I am hearing whispers and rumours of an infiltration by foreign spies. Normally I would not be concerned but tomorrow is important. *Vitally* important."

"I understand Sir and I too have heard the rumours. I am still checking, but at this moment I have no reason to suspect a threat. Probably just more Ukrainian disinformation."

"Probably," the President agreed, "Call me if anything changes. Good night."

Sokolov sat back in his chair and lit another cigarette, staring at the ceiling. Perhaps he *should* be starting to worry.

***

After leaving the service station, they drove a few miles past S Yedrovo before taking a farm track into the woods beside the highway. Headlights extinguished the men had tried to rest but only Adam had actually slept. Eventually his snores became too much and Paweł had punched him in the ribs, "As if the smell of your feet wasn't bad enough you noisy bastard!"

The scuffle that followed was good natured, but the sound of their grunts and laughs woke the rest of the team as they stumbled out of their car, to find Paweł and Adam wrestling in the dust. The men all joined in, enjoying the relief of a brief moment of silliness, their laughter surprisingly loud in the darkness of the tress. Wojciech suddenly realised just how much tension the team had been carrying since their arrival in Ukraine - and that it was about to get a lot worse.

Chapter Thirty-One

They resumed the last leg of the drive a few hours before dawn, driving slowly towards the village of Valday.

"Now we just need to steal a boat," said Wojciech.

"Stealing vehicles is becoming a bit of a habit, eh Chief?" Ksiądz grinned, "Maybe we can try for a helicopter next time?"

Tomasz and Wojciech laughed along.

"Maybe you better pray for his forgiveness too, eh Ksiądz?" asked Tomasz.

The laughter intensified, although Wojciech detected the note of tension creeping in again. It seemed hard to believe this insane journey had begun less than two days earlier.

The team abandoned the cars behind an old factory at the edge of the sleeping village, walking the rest of the way to the Lake Valdai shoreline. They darted through the black shadows which inhabited the space between sporadic streetlights, scanning each gateway and door for potential trouble. Occasionally a dog barked somewhere in the distance or a light burned dimly in a cottage window, but mostly the night was a thick blanket of silence broken only by their hurried footsteps and muffled clanking of their packs.

"There," said Adam pointing towards a small jetty that stretched out into the lake. Four or five small boats were tied up alongside, bobbing gently on the rippled water.

"Move," Wojciech whispered. Paweł, Tomasz and Adam ran for a small thicket of trees while Ksiądz weaved his way to the wooden pier. He glanced into each boat before jumping into a small, white vessel that was only just large enough to fit five men and their equipment. He began loosening the painter ropes while one-by-one the rest of the team ran along the jetty and jumped onboard. Their boots sounded thunderously loud as they clattered along the rough hewn planks. Wojciech was sure someone would hear them at any moment and raise the alarm. There would be no escape this close to Leontin's backyard.

Paweł was the last to embark and Ksiądz thrust a pair of wooden oars at him, grinning, "The first couple of hundred metres has to be done by hand."

Paweł swore, but set to work, pulling the boat away from shore as quickly and quietly as possible. He swore even more loudly when Ksiądz proceeded to splash the boat, and him, with holy water.

"Haven't you run out yet?" he growled.

"*Nie*," Ksiądz's smile grew wider as he leaned over the side and refilled the hip flask from the chilly water below.

They pulled away from shore, the only sound was the muffled splash of the oars and Paweł's laboured breathing which hung around his head like a cloud of pale white smoke. Adam sat in the back of the boat scanning the shoreline and houses behind through his night scope, watching for any sign that they had been spotted - or were being followed. After a few minutes he raised an open hand. "Thank God," puffed Paweł, shipping the oars.

"I told you every man in a combat situation becomes a believer," Ksiądz winked. He pulled the ripcord on the outboard and the men held their breath as the motor coughed, and burst into life. Using the handheld GPS he steered the boat on a north-easterly course, heading towards a group of thinly wooded islands. Above them, the sky began to lighten and the temperature fell a few degrees, causing a low mist to form across the surface of the water. Off to the right an Orthodox Church sat in the middle of a monastery compound, its gilded onion domes pointing their way to the heavens.

"Let's hope the monks are still sleeping," grinned Adam.

"I hope they are awake and praying for us," whispered Tomasz, crossing himself.

"*I'm* praying for us," Ksiądz said, crossing himself and kissing the silver crucifix that hung around his neck. The boat was now headed directly for one of the islands.

"Put us on the beach over there," Wojciech said to Ksiądz, pointing to a patch of reeds ahead, "Run her up into the mud."

The boat slid up the sloping shore and Paweł leaped out on point. He ran ahead into the treeline and took up a covering position. The rest of the team followed quickly behind him.

"What do we do with the boat?" asked Ksiądz, "Will we be coming back this way?"

"No, but we should hide it to avoid attracting

unwanted attention," Wojciech instructed. Ksiądz and Adam dragged the boat clear of the water and into a patch of thorny brush.

"That'll do," called Paweł, "You can't see it."

"*Dobrze*. Time to change again then," said Wojciech reaching into his pack and retrieving a black wetsuit. The rest of the team followed his lead, changing into their own wetsuits and stuffing clothes back into their packs which went into waterproof bags.

A few minutes later they were moving silently through the trees, and before long they could see another body of water glinting in the dawn sunlight ahead. Wojciech called a halt and pointed, "There's about 800 metres of water between us and the compound. Just a quick swim between us and the asset."

Adam scanned the far shoreline, "There's a perimeter fence running along the lake edge and a few guards making rounds, but I can't see any incursion detection devices. Or dogs."

"Thank God," muttered Paweł, "I hate dogs."

"There will be dogs in there somewhere. Leontin is a dog man," Adam cautioned, "There's also a large boom running across the water in front of the Dacha. No way we're getting over that unseen."

"We'll head for that cluster of trees on the waterline at the northern end of the barrier," Wojciech pointed again, "Once we're across, Ksiądz can cut through the fence. Then we'll move south east along this track to join the main service road," Wojciech traced a route on his GPS screen ending at a large, grey square. "The Dacha where Leontin is having his meeting is this building here."

"Lots of trees, lots of cover," Tomasz commented.

"We're going in wearing our Federal Protection Service uniforms," grinned Wojciech, "So cover is useful but not essential. We'll look like just another detail assigned to the President. After we get through the fence, we'll make our way to one of the outbuildings here, then wait until the meeting starts. As soon as we're sure everyone is present, we're going to march our way to the main building."

"Ballsy," laughed Tomasz, "I like it."

"As far as we can tell, the VIP will arrive by helicopter at the airbase north west of the Dacha compound and then be driven down for the meeting.

"Adam, I want you to make straight for the woods opposite the Dacha. The slope should allow you to cover the entrance, the access road and any vehicles parked out front. You can then advise us when Leontin and his guest arrive."

"*Tak*. We don't want your smelly feet giving Leontin advance notice of our arrival," Paweł added, earning a swift blow to the arm for his trouble.

"*Dobrze*," Adam nodded.

Wojciech continued to point at buildings and landmarks on the electronic map as he talked, "We'll go in through the front door here. Paweł and I will locate and secure Leontin. Tomasz and Ksiądz, I need you to find and disable the facility's comms which appear to be located in this building," he pointed at a small two storey structure topped by a tower of some kind, hidden in the trees south of the Dacha, "When you're sure everything is disabled, I want you to appropriate a vehicle befitting the President of the Russian Federation and meet us back at the main entrance. We'll collect Adam and drive straight out through the Dacha compound gate here and on through the airbase until we reach the public road. We have to get this right because there's only one road in and out, so no doubling back if something goes wrong.

"Once we come out of the staging point, we have to move fast. The Russians will figure out something is wrong eventually, but not before the meeting is due to end. We should have about 60 minutes to grab Leontin and get out of the compound. That's our head start and we have to make every second count."

Wojciech took a moment to study the faces of his team. They all wore the same steely look and determined grin, ready to do him, and the Fatherland, proud. These were some of the bravest men Wojciech had ever met - and there was a very good chance that he was marching them to their deaths.

Ksiądz clapped him on the shoulder, "It's OK boss, we got this. Let's go arrest President Leontin."

***

As Ksiądz and Adam slid into the water, Tomasz called HQ to confirm they were on final approach. Seconds later he, Wojciech and Paweł were following into the chilly, black waters of Lake Valdai. Above them, the sky was clouding over, obscuring the early morning sun as a strengthening wind whipped waves around the swimmers. Despite the conditions, they made good time, arriving at the opposite bank in less than fifteen minutes. Obscured by the waterfront trees, Ksiądz snipped at the fence with a pair of wire cutters. Adam squatted by his side providing cover while the three men waited in the water. They peeled the fence apart, taking it in turns to crawl through the hole and jog across the perimeter track into the thicker trees beyond.

Wetsuits were replaced by fatigues bearing FSO badges, before being placed back into one of the waterproof bags. Tomasz climbed a tree and tied the holdall securely to a branch where it was hidden by the leaves. "Who knew climbing telephone polls was a transferable skill? Maybe I do owe my brother-in-law something after all!" he laughed, jumping back down to the ground.

Moving back onto the track, they followed the razor-topped fence south east, skirting around a red tennis court and assorted small buildings nestled in the trees. A single lane access road ran parallel to the path, thankfully very quiet at this time of day.

After a few hundred metres, Wojciech led the men off the track and into woods. A thick cushion of pine needles underfoot absorbed the noise around them and Wojciech finally understood why Stalin had found the silence of Dolgiye Borody unnerving. Through the leaves of the surrounding conifer trees, the gabled roof of the Dacha could be glimpsed, its central pyramid-shaped skylight pointing towards the overcast heavens above. A minute or so later, they halted outside a small log cabin. Paweł glanced through a window, taking in the dust and mouse dropping that covered the floor. He nodded. Not only was the building empty, but it didn't look like anyone would be using it any time soon either. Tomasz pushed the door and it swung open easily, revealing a collection of stacked garden furniture and various tools laid out neatly on a workbench. Apparently it was some kind of workshop used by the groundskeeper.

Wojciech nodded to Adam and the sniper melted back into the trees, heading towards the access road. Inside the cabin, Paweł took up a firing position, covering the woods back in the direction they had just come. The kapitan moved to the other window at the back of the cabin, studying the Dacha beyond. It was large, modern and completely lacking in character, like an American chain hotel. Each floor had several deep balconies and verandahs, each enclosed by white columns, with windows set well back - probably in an attempt to protect the notoriously paranoid Leontin from would-be assassins. As he studied the Dacha, Wojciech also noticed that an SPB officer would stride into sight periodically, shrugging off the boredom of another watch on sentry duty.

"Adam is safely across the road," Paweł whispered.

"Let's hope he can find a good vantage point," Wojciech said, shifting attention to the small wooded hill that lay opposite the Dacha where Adam would be lying in wait.

Tomasz and Ksiądz unstacked a few of the chairs, trying to make themselves comfortable while they waited. "You bring us to all the best places, *kapitan*" Ksiądz laughed.

"Why does everywhere we go smell like Adam's feet?" Paweł asked.

"Still better than Kandahar," muttered Tomasz, pulling his cap low and closing his eyes.

Chapter Thirty-Two

The tension in the Warsaw control room was unbearable, like a heavy weight pushing down on the operations team. In theory they were there to direct the operation and provide support, but Grabowski knew there was nothing they could do, they were merely greedy onlookers waiting to witness a disaster. Everywhere jaws clenched and brows sweated, the temperature rising along with the musky smell of unwashed bodies, stress and stale coffee. There had been a moment of jubilation as they watched the red dots crossed the fence surrounding the Dacha compound on screen. But the oppressive atmosphere quickly returned as the watchers waited for the team to make their move.

Grabowski knew exactly how high the stakes were, but Błaszcak has still felt the need to remind him, "If those men are captured and identified as Polish, we might just trigger the start of World War 3."

"And you don't think we're already engaged in Cold War 2? Have some faith please sir," Grabowski countered, "everything is proceeding to plan."

"For now," the politician muttered.

***

The silence was broken by the sound of a vehicle convoy arriving at the north gate to Leontin's compound. "I hear four engines," said Tomasz, "Nothing major though. SUVs?"

Right on cue, Adam radioed through, "Four SUVs in close formation heading towards the Dacha."

"Then I think our primary target has arrived," said Wojciech scanning the area with his binoculars, "Comms check."

Each man sounded off in turn as they double-checked their gear.

"Visual confirmation of the Target," Adam's voice came through their earpieces, "Are you sure you don't want me to take him?"

"No, stand down," Wojciech said, "Just monitor the situation and let me know if anything changes."

"Two guards escorted Leontin into the Dacha and took up station at the front door. The others are waiting in the SUVs, parked opposite the driveway at the main entrance."

In the distance the sound of an approaching helicopter could be heard echoing between the trees.

"That will be Leontin's guest arriving at the heliport. Adam, let us know when he arrives at the Dacha and we'll move in," said Wojciech. The team crouched in nervous silence for several minutes, primed and ready to move. Eventually, a second convoy of SUVs drove down the access road.

"Confirm VIP arrival," Adam reported, "Cannot identify the individual. Older male, white hair flanked by two bodyguards in black suits."

"Keep us updated. Out." Wojciech gave Leontin and his guest another five minutes to get settled then led his men out the cabin, marching quickly through the trees towards the Dacha. They rounded the corner of the building just in time to see a group of men in black suits usher a white haired man from a large black vehicle and in through the main door of the dacha.

"Sixty minutes, starting now," said Wojciech, each man starting the countdown on his watch, "*Powodzenia* my friends."

Chapter Thirty-Three

```
>> sudo .op_cellkill
>> destination_range -i > 156.34.251.0/254
>> op_cellkill initiated…
>> sending remote activation command…
>> bot_cluster_1 ack
>> bot_cluster_2 ack
>> bot_cluster_3 ack
>> bot_cluster_4 ack
>> bot_cluster_5 ack
>> …
>> …
>> …
```

***

And with that, a global network of malware infected computers had been activated. Each bot generating a stream of continuous requests directed at a seemingly random range of devices based in Russia. Within minutes the targets were overwhelmed, unable to handle the millions of data packets being received and acknowledged every second. Moments later they would fail completely, taking a subsection of the Russian cellphone network offline.

***

Agent Agnieszka stood behind Piotr, leaning on the back of his chair so she could peer over his shoulder – and because she knew it made him nervous. White numbers quickly scrolled across his laptop screen but she had no idea what she was looking at. "What is happening? Is it working?"

"Yes," Piotr sighed, looking up at her like she was some kind of idiot, "It's working. The target network is down. I hope you have the other $250k ready."

She hit the speed dial on her cellphone, speaking a single word when the call was answered, "Go."

***

"ABW confirms the cellular network is down in the Dolgiye Borody district," one of the operators called out, "We're good to go."

"Is there any way to confirm the network is down?" Błaszyk asked nervously.

"No sir, not without showing ourselves to the Russians. We must assume the Ukrainian hackers are as good as they claim."

"They bloody better be for half a million dollars," Grabowski growled. He tapped his smartphone screen then turned his attention back to the operation centre projections.

***

Tomasz's satphone buzzed, a new one word message from control:

***

Matka > IŚĆ

Chapter Thirty-Four

Adam had found a suitable position on the hillside, where he had a clear view of the Dacha and a little of the access road in each direction. He had moved a few branches to create a little hollow where he could lay, then spread a camouflage net to create a makeshift hide that would deter most casual observers. Below him, several security men clustered around the SUVs a few metres from him at the base of the wooded slope. Out of sight of the Dacha door, they chatted and smoked, apparently expecting to be waiting for some time.

After a while one of the men walked into the trees, the jeers of the his colleagues echoing off the trunks around him. He continued walking, straight towards where Adam was lying on the ground, concealed under a camouflage net. "Are you in position?" Wojciech's voice buzzed in his ear.

With so many hostiles nearby, he couldn't risk using the sniper rifle. Even with a suppressor, the sound of a shot would give his position away. Besides, the man would almost certainly see the barrel moving as it poked through the netting and the whole point of him being here was to not be spotted.

"Adam, are you in position?" Wojciech was

becoming more insistent, but there was no way for him to answer.

Smoothly, silently, the sniper slowed his breath and reached for his knife, tensing his body, ready to spring if the man got too close. Adam would have to time his jump perfectly if he was to disable the man before he could draw his gun - and even then, it wasn't likely to be a killing blow.

"Adam? Come in, over." He prayed the man couldn't hear the radio.

Finally, the security man stopped a metre short of Adam and unzipped his black suit pants. He groaned in relief as he urinated, while the sniper watched his every movement, alert to the chance that the man may spot him at any moment. The man stared at the bushes ahead and Adam was sure he had been discovered. But after a few minutes, the security man finished and headed back to the SUVs, never realising just how close he had come to dying.

When he was sure the man had reached the bottom of the slope, Adam relaxed, feeling the tension drain from his muscles as he sank back onto the ground. He shifted his weight a little, then turned his attention back to the rifle and the action below, "All clear Wojciech, you're good to go."

***

The four man team marched in steady formation along the access road towards the sweeping drive that led to the building where their target waited. Wojciech scanned the many balconies and windows of the three storey building, taking note of the various security surveillance devices mounted on the walls. In the distance, armed soldiers crossed and re-crossed the carefully manicured lawns on the look out for intruders or other potential threats.

The curved drive way led up to a glass roofed canopy where the two soldiers guarding the main entrance had been joined by a pair of men in black suits. However, the sight of their SPB badged uniforms and a quick salute were enough to gain access to the building. Bringing up the rear, Paweł gestured to the four guards to follow him into the wood-panelled entrance hall.

None of the men noticed they had been encircled by Wojciech, Tomasz and Ksiądz, nor the electric shock batons they were holding, until it was too late. The sounds of crackling electricity echoed around the foyer, followed by three unconscious bodies crumpling to the polished marble floor. The fourth man was faster though, drawing his pistol and pointing it at Tomasz. There was a stunned silence for a fraction of a second as the two men stared each other, broken by the sound of lightly breaking glass followed simultaneously by two thuds.

Then the man stumbled backwards, as though he had received a powerhouse blow to the gut. He fell to the ground, gun in hand, a look of horror and pain etched on his face, a river of crimson pouring from his back. He had been shot. Twice.

Wojciech turned and saluted his gratitude to the trees opposite, noting the two holes punched in the bulletproof glass at the front of the building. He couldn't see Adam, but he knew he was there somewhere - thank God.

The three incapacitated guards were dragged out of the hall and into a sitting room off to one side. Each was bound hand and foot with cable ties then piled behind a sofa out of sight. The body of the fourth guard was bundled into a small cleaning closet to the left of the front door. Ksiądz and Paweł hurriedly mopped at the bloodstained marble floor, trying to remove any trace of what had just happened. Meanwhile, Tomasz swung his baton at the ceiling mounted CCTV cameras, plastic and circuitry raining down onto the floor. The less evidence they left behind, the better.

An impressive double staircase led to the upper floors, a luxurious green carpeted trail to Leontin's guest rooms above. There were several rooms leading off from the entryway, a plush office cum library, lounges, a large dining room with enormous polished wooden table and chairs arranged under a glittering crystal chandelier.

"Country house? This place is a palace," Tomasz whispered incredulously.

"Even more plush than the Archbishop of Gniezo's," Ksiądz joked.

As they moved silently through the house they came across another soldier - black suit pairing stationed outside one of the doors. Without slowing his pace, Wojciech marched his men confidently towards the guards.

The Russian sentry challenged him, "*Prival. Vkhod zapreshchen.*"

"*Da, da,*" nodded Wojciech, showing his hands, palms up.

"Not today, pal," added Paweł appearing from behind Wojciech. He pointed a suppressed pistol at the two guards while Tomasz waved his electronic shock baton menacingly, "No one else has to die today, so let's go inside, shall we?"

Wojciech turned and saluted once more to the trees

opposite. With the guards now under control, Tomasz and Ksiądz moved off to find the comms building. Wojciech bent down, relieving the bleeding man of his radio earpiece.

"Ready?" asked Paweł.

"Ready," nodded Wojciech. They pushed the large panelled door open, prodding the two guards ahead of them with their assault rifles. Inside the room was dominated by a large glass wall that ran the entire length of the property, offering a view out across Lake Valdai to the island monastery beyond. Backs to the door, two men sat in in large over-stuffed armchairs in front of the window, talking quietly. Vladimir Leontin was on the far side facing the door, his profile visible against the light outside. He turned to see what was causing the commotion at the door, his face showing shock as he spotted the blood-soaked guard, but his eyes burned with pure rage. The white-haired man sat with his back to Wojciech, stopped talking when he saw Leontin's look.

"Many apologies for the interruption gentlemen, but we're here for the President," said Wojciech, "If you wouldn't mind standing up and walking slowly towards me, we'll be out of your way as quickly as possible."

"And exactly which president were you looking for?" the white-haired man asked, rising unsteadily to his feet and turning to face the intruders.

Paweł whistled, "Joe Blyden is the VIP?"

Chapter Thirty-Five

Although they had had satellite images to familiarise them with the general layout of the Dacha compound, Warsaw could not locate any plans for the Dacha internals. When Leontin had had the estate rebuilt, secrecy was at the top of his wish list. Tomasz and Ksiądz found an external door in one of the lounges with a set of stairs leading out the south side of the house, almost directly into the trees. No sentries in sight, they made a quick sprint into the forest, the blanket of pine needles absorbing all sound once again. The two men weaved between trees, skirting carefully around a cluster of low buildings arranged around a central square. The tower on top of the comms building could be seen rising above the trees just ahead.

Surprisingly, the door to the building was unguarded so Tomasz and Ksiądz simply marched through it into a medium-sized office. The room was lined with desks and computers, staffed by several uniformed operators.

"*Ne dvigaytes!*" Ksiądz yelled, pointing his gun at the startled men and women inside, motioning them to move backwards. Each reluctantly raised their hands, then stood and moved towards the back of the room. Ksiądz waited until they had all turned to face the wall before securing their hands with cable ties. "Now what?" he asked Tomasz.

"You cover them while I sort out the comms," Tomasz replied, seating himself at one of the computer terminals. For a few minutes the only sound was the clatter of the keyboard as he manually disabled the network replication failover, then began to take each of the Dacha's digital communications channels offline. Satisfied, he stood up and walked to a sound-proofed door at the opposite end of the room. As he opened it, the roaring sound of powerful air conditioning exploded outwards. Tomasz walked in and spent another few minutes quickly and systematically hacking at the wires trailing out of each of the server racks with his combat knife, ensuring both power and network connectivity could not be easily restored. He double-checked that everything had been disconnected, kicking a few of the servers and network switches for good measure. Then he nodded to himself and went back to the doorway.

"Bring them in here," Tomasz said, gesturing to the Russians. Ksiądz did as he was asked, herding the comms team into the air conditioned room, locking and securing the door behind them. Tomasz smashed the electric keypad next to the door with his baton then delivered a burst of electricity to its internals, shorting the locking circuit. With no way to override the electronic locks, the comms officers would be trapped for some time, delaying any attempt to restore communications or raise the alarm with the outside world. They piled a few desks in front of the door for good measure, just in case someone tried kicking it down.

"Network is offline," Ksiądz said into his radio.

"Confirmed," Wojciech's voice crackled back.

Tomasz led Ksiądz back out into the corridor and up four flights of stairs where a door blocked their progress. He kicked until the frame splintered and the door flew open, revealing a flat roof beyond. "Those have to go too," Tomasz said, gesturing with his knife at an array of satellite dishes and a cell tower.

"Quietly?" asked Ksiądz, plucking a hand grenade from his webbing and waving it at Tomasz hopefully.

"Quietly," Tomasz nodded, turning his attention to a waist-high, grey junction box that leaned against the wall of the stairwell. An ominous electrical hum vibrated from inside.

With Ksiądz's help, he pried the door of the box open, exposing a collection of neatly coiled power cables and above them, an array of heavy duty switches. Ksiądz moved to the edge of the roof watching the road below while Tomasz flicked each power switch inside the cabinet. Then he smashed them all with the butt of his rifle for good measure. The humming stopped immediately. Confident mains electricity was no longer flowing, he thrust his shock baton into the cabinet, one million volts of direct current overloading the delicate network circuitry. The acrid smell of burning electrics and melting plastic evidence that nothing on the roof of the building would be coming back online any time soon.

"*Dobrze*," Tomasz grinned, "All the comms are down. Now you better find us some wheels."

Ksiądz nodded and jogged down the stairs.

"Comms are offline," Tomasz broadcast to his comrades from the roof, watching Ksiądz flit from tree to tree, working his way back to the cluster of small buildings they had passed earlier.

***

Paweł pulled out his phone and began to record a video, "It's not every day you get to meet two world leaders, is it? Say 'cheese'."

The two presidents glowered at him.

"You're here to negotiate peace?" Wojciech asked, worried that he may have just accidentally committed the gravest error, causing secret peace talks to break down and extending the war in Ukraine.

"No, I'm here for the ice cream," Blyden smiled condescendingly, "There's so much more here at stake than you realise. So stand down, soldier, I'm here to negotiate a new *war*."

"We're not interested in a war on our border thanks Chief," said Paweł, "So if it's all the same to you, we'll just take Vlad and be heading off."

"You don't understand, man. We need Leontin and we need this war. *You* need this war. Eventually we can pull back in Ukraine, but first we need to reinforce the threat of wider conflict. Why else do you think NATO has been expanding? Two years ago it was a toothless force without a reason to exist. Now, everyone wants in - and military spend is way up. A war is exactly what we need to get our post-shutdown world back on track We'll restore order and rebuild our economies - unless you want to live under Chinese rule? Unless you miss communism that badly?" Blyden arched his eyebrow questioningly. He even looked like a stereotypical cartoon bad guy.

"I wasn't even *born* when the Berlin Wall came down," muttered Paweł.

"So your plan is to start a new Cold War, working with a man charged with war crimes? Forget invading neighbouring states, this guy, this *monster*, forcibly removes Ukrainian children from their families for brainwashing." Wojciech was becoming angrier by the second.

"Well, y'know.... kids," Blyden grinned weirdly.

"Enough," said Wojciech, thoroughly creeped out, "Paweł, get the safe room ready."

Paweł pocketed his phone and reached under Leontin's desk to press a button mounted on the underside. A section of wall opposite the window slid open, revealing a hidden safe room. He entered the shiny steel-lined chamber and used a screwdriver to remove an access panel beside the door. First, he shorted the intercom circuits, ensuring that no one inside could call for help. Next, he overrode the internal door release mechanism so that once activated, the lock could not be opened electronically from inside or outside. He made one more sweep of the tiny room to check for hidden weapons or tools, then called "Clear!"

Coming back into the room, he stood close enough to Wojciech to whisper, "Are we going to take Blyden too?"

Wojciech thought for a moment, "As much as I want to, he's too frail and would slow us down. Is he even physically fit enough to make a mad dash for the border?" he paused again. "No, we can't take the risk."

Paweł nodded once in agreement.

"Gentlemen, if you please, into the safe room - and you too Mr President. Make yourselves comfortable - I am hoping you will be in there for several hours."

Leontin began edging his way with the other three men. "Uh, uh, not you, Vlad, the other president," Wojciech shook his head and waved some cable ties, "I've brought you some jewellery."

"You're crazy," said Leontin, "You'll never get away with this. You and your men are going to die."

"Possibly Vlad, but you'd better hope not."

Paweł herded the interpreters, guards and President into the safe room.

"Damn polacks," Blyden cursed.

"Slava Ukraini, *kurwa*," Paweł replied, slamming the door behind Blyden. He then took the cable ties from Wojciech and laced them around Leontin's wrists. Tight. This was followed by a cloth gag to keep him quiet.

"Can we give him just a little shock? Please?" Paweł grinned. Leontin's eyes widened.

"No, I don't want to have to carry him," Wojciech checking the safe room door was locked, "Are we ready?"

"Ready," said Paweł grabbing Leontin's shoulder and steering him towards the hallway, "Come on Vlad, you've got a date with a judge."

"Asset secured, repeat, asset secured. Now moving to the rendezvous point," Wojciech announced over his comms headset. He checked his watch, they were still ahead of schedule. Perhaps they *could* pull this off.

Chapter Thirty-Six

"What is this place?" Pushkin asked as the helicopter streaked low across a lake and past an onion-domed monastery. They were headed towards a small cluster of red-roofed buildings surrounded by a serious-looking fence clinging to the shoreline. He could see soldiers moving between the trees, but he was sure this was no regular base.

"It's called Dolgiye Borody and it's a private dacha of the President of the Russian Federation." Ovechkin explained, "It was built by Stalin in the early 1930s but he couldn't stand the silence of the area. Leontin loves it though, almost as much as he loves to show it off to his closest allies when he has the chance."

"Not many chances since the sanctions, I'm guessing," Pushkin said with a wry smile.

"Uh sir," the pilot called from the cockpit, "I'm not getting a response on the radio."

"We can't wait for clearance," Ovechkin yelled back, "get us on the ground *now*."

Surely the Poles couldn't be here already. Could they?

"Let's hope they don't have automated anti-aircraft defences," the pilot muttered.

***

Tomasz came marching smartly through the Dacha door, grinning like a demented badger. He saluted Wojciech and bowed theatrically to Leontin. Gripping his bound wrists, Wojciech steered the president towards the front of the front while Paweł moved quickly ahead to ensure the hallway and ground floor rooms were still clear.

Wojciech glanced out the window and saw an armoured troop carrier approaching the entrance. Tomasz and Paweł tracked its progress with their rifles, readying themselves for a team of elite Russian soldiers to come piling out of the back door.

The vehicle stopped under the glass canopy and the two men were relieved when Ksiądz leaped from the driver's door. "Welcome to the Tigr, gentlemen," he said grinning, "When only the best will do for our presidential guest." Paweł and Tomasz grabbed Leontin under the arms and bundled him through the rear doors of the Tigr, before jumping in behind him. Wojciech was last to board, pulling the rear doors closed behind him. He scrambled over the seats to join Ksiądz in the front of the vehicle.

"It's not sexy but the windows are high enough to prevent most people looking in," Ksiądz continued his introduction, "But most importantly, it has 5mm thick armour plating which may come in handy."

His commentary was interrupted by the sound of another helicopter flying fast and low overhead. Clearly it was coming in to land at the airbase too. "We really need to go. Now," said Wojciech, clapping Ksiądz on the shoulder, before speaking into his radio, "Adam, we're on our way to you." He looked out the window once more at the palatial Dacha and wondered what other dodgy deals had been negotiated within its walls.

Ksiądz steered the Tigr down the sloping driveway and back on to the service road that wound through the compound. Adam came sprinting out of the trees, SVDM slung across his back and Tomasz threw the rear door open, helping to pull the sniper inside. The personnel carrier then turned north west and drove to the gate of the Dacha compound as quickly as possible without drawing attention to themselves. Wojciech felt like his body was humming, nervous tension ready to explode like static lightning bolts from his fingertips and scalp. Leontin was pushed flat onto the floor of the vehicle, a collection of kit bags and equipment piled roughly on top of him, making him invisible.

As before, the guards on the gate showed minimal interest in the vehicle or its occupants. Probably because they were heading from an ultra-secure compound to an airbase full of soldiers he guessed. Ksiądz handed over a sheaf of papers and grunted a vague greeting, but after a cursory glance, the sentry waved them on. They passed a barracks building on their right along with a scattering of administrative blocks and workshops. As they neared the helicopter landing pads, a light transport vehicle swerved across the road in front of them, heading towards the Dacha. As the vehicle accelerated past, Wojciech glimpsed a wild-haired figure in the passenger seat, something vaguely familiar about the grim look of determination in the man's face.

Two helicopters could be seen on the concrete landing pads, then they were at the perimeter fence. Ksiądz repeated the bureaucratic dance, passing a thick sheaf of papers for the sentry on the gate to ignore. His colleague did a quick walk-round of the Tigr, then waved them through the gate.

Tomasz made a loud, theatrical sigh of relief, and the team laughed, but the smiles never quite reached their eyes. Ksiądz was completely focused on driving, steering the Tigr through a small country village, skirting around the shore of Lake Valdai and making for the M10 highway once more.

As soon as they left the compound, the road was swallowed up by trees, helping to keep the stolen Tigr invisible from any air patrols. Ksiądz hoped they didn't meet any military traffic or roadblocks, at least not between here and the highway. In the same way that there there was only one road to the Dacha, there was only one in and out of Dolgiye Borody too. If they were stopped, the mission would be over. If they were stopped, they would be *dead*. The sooner they could get to the highway, the better.

Wojciech hauled Leontin off the floor and pushed him onto one of the benches that ran along both sides of the Tigr's interior. "This is for you, Mr President," he said, activating a button-sized tracking beacon and pinning it under the man's shirt collar.

"Now can I zap him?" asked Paweł, waving his shock baton and grinning dementedly.

***

Every eye in the the Warsaw control room had been staring at team's satellite trackers for hours, the red beacons zigging and zagging across the compound as each man set about his part of the mission at the Dacha. Now, against the odds, all five had regrouped and somehow made it out of the compound and away from the Dolgiye Borody peninsula. But when the red dots were joined by a single yellow triangle, the room erupted into excited cheering and clapping.

Right on cue, the phone rang, "We have the asset," said Tomasz.

"Good luck gentlemen," said Grabowski, "God be with you."

They had already completed one impossible task, the General thought. Now they just had to do a second - escape the entire Russian army.

"One more thing sir," added Tomasz, "When we took him, the asset had a guest."

"Yes, that's what out intel told us. Were there any problems?"

"Yes," Tomasz replied, "Leontin's guest was The President of the United States of America."

A murmur of shock and disbelief passed through the control room. "Say again," Grabowski said. Behind him, the colour drained from Błaszyk's face, thinking that the mission he had suggested and sanctioned may have just become a diplomatic crisis, "They are sure it was him? The real Blyden, not some trick by Leontin? An imposter of some kind?"

"No, no tricks sir. *The* Joe Blyden was in Dolgiye Borody meeting with the asset," Tomasz repeated, "Just to be clear, this was not a peace negotiation or any kind of attempt to end the war. He was meeting Leontin to talk about *extending* it."

The background murmurings grew louder. Surely this could not be true, but Błaszyk sighed with relief - he was off the hook, his crazy suggestion had worked. For now.

Grabowski turned and motioned for silence, "Understood. Proceed as planned to the extraction point." He ended the call, feeling a dark rage ignite deep inside his soul. Now all his men had to do was escape the entire Russian army *and* Poland's so-called allies.

He turned to Błaszyk, "I believe this is what the Americans call a FUBAR."

Chapter Thirty-Seven

As soon as he arrived at the Dacha, Ovechkin knew something was wrong. He pushed the large door open and walked into the empty entry hall, his feet echoing on the polished marble floor. Where the hell were the sentries? Obviously the President had wanted to keep this meeting as low key as possible for some reason, but he would never have left the entrance unguarded. Every official property in Russia has visible security at the entrance, even the most secret presidential residences. He leaned into the tiny sentry niche next to the door and grabbed the phone sat on the desk. He was going to call Chernov in Moscow and let him know how badly the Alexey and the SPB had screwed up, but the phone line was dead.

For the first time since starting this operation in Moscow Ovechkin felt uncertainty, that perhaps the gang of men he was chasing were smarter than he thought. His uneasiness deepened when he realised that he too would be facing a firing squad if he didn't figure out what was going on.

A groan from the sitting room off to the left snapped him back to the present. Walking around the furniture he discovered the missing sentries and two other men in black suits lying in a crumpled heap. One guard was nursing a swollen and bleeding temple, the other still unconscious. All four men had been bound hand and foot with cable ties. Ovechkin grabbed the half-awake sentry and shook him by the collar of his uniform, demanding, "Where. Is. The. President?"

Pushkin cut the ties securing the Russians, then helped Ovechkin drag the conscious soldier to his feet. Unsure who they were, the two men in suits were left in place. Leaning heavily on Pushkin, the sentry led the FSB men along the corridor that led under the stairs, away from the foyer. "The President is in here," he said weakly.

Ovechkin pounded the polished wooden door with his fist, "Mr President," he called loudly, "are you safe and well?" There was no response. He tried once more, before pushing the door open. The large room was empty, two armchairs turned to face the enormous picture window and the view out across the lake. It was certainly impressive and Ovechkin found himself staring at the luxurious fixtures and sumptuous furnishings for a little too long. The opulence of the Dacha was not what he expected of his President, a man who had spent decades cultivating a careful image of spartan masculinity.

"Where is he?" Pushkin demanded of the soldier.

"I don't know sir," the man stammered, "perhaps he is in the safe room?" He led them to the back wall and slid a wooden panelled partition aside to reveal a polished metal door behind. Ovechkin pushed past to repeat his door-pounding yelling routine on the reinforced steel. Again, there was no response.

"Sir!" said the soldier, "Sir! The room is sound-proofed and can only be opened from the inside. If the internal intercom is broken you can't hear them and they can't hear you. *If* the President is in there, he will come out when *he* is sure it is safe for him to do so."

"Fine," said Ovechkin angrily, "I'm sure the President is perfectly safe and well in there. But I still want an immediate search of the Dacha compound *and* the helicopter base for anything strange or out of place. And I want a team to get this door open. Now!"

***

The Poles were making good time on the highway when they had a stroke of good luck, encountering a convoy of military trucks heading north at speed. According to briefing intel Grabowski had shown them, the Russians were sending troops to strengthen the north western border with Finland following their successful NATO membership application. Ksiądz merged with the column, pleased to note their's wasn't the only Tigr in the line.

"How long until they notice they have an extra vehicle in the convoy?" Adam asked Wojciech, "And how are we going to detach ourselves when the time comes?"

"I doubt we will be unnoticed forever," the team leader replied, "But we'll use it while we can."

"Once the FSO or whoever realise he's gone, they're going to throw everything at finding us," said Paweł jerking a thumb in Leontin's direction, "And sooner or later someone will notice the Tigr missing from the compound."

"*Tak*, we're on borrowed time. Which is why we all need to remain alert and observant," Wojciech nodded as the team sank into silence. He scratched his chin thoughtfully. Back in Wrocław, the plan had been to collect Leontin and make a break for the nearest border - Latvia.

But that was also the most obvious plan of action. When the Russians realised what had happened at the dacha it would be a straight race to see who reached the border first. And it was unlikely to be them. There was also the question of how they would actually cross a heavily defended border without getting killed.

Grabowski had suggested an alternative which they had both dismissed as fantasy. Instead of heading west, they could instead go north and make for Estonia or maybe even Finland. Such a route would take them close to, or even past, St Petersburg - a veritable suicide mission. But the sheer recklessness of the plan meant that their pursuers probably wouldn't even consider it either.

Wojciech scratched again at his stubble and sighed. He had to make a decision soon, but the convoy would buy them some time until he made up his mind.

Chapter Thirty-Eight

The Dolgiye Borody base commander had arrived with his engineers to open the safe room door and was working hard to placate an increasingly irate Ovechkin. Technically the SPB was responsible for providing close protection for the President, but his men - he - was responsible for defending the perimeter of the long peninsula on which the Dacha stood. "We have tried contacting Moscow, but the comms system has been sabotaged. Even the local cellular tower is out," he said, "We're on our own for now."

Ovechkin checked his mobile phone to discover he had no signal. "The safe room door, can we blow it off? A small shaped charge?" he demanded.

"Like you see in the movies? Of course not, no. We would kill everyone inside. We must cut our way through."

The engineers set to work with a circular cutting saw, orange sparks spraying across the sumptuous sitting room, bouncing off the priceless furniture and scorching the deep pile woollen carpet. Ovechkin and the base commander moved out to the safety of the corridor to talk.

"How do we raise the alarm?" the commander asked Ovechkin.

"*Should* we raise the alarm?" Ovechkin asked quietly, "As far as we know, the President is behind that door."

"As far as we know…"

"So we keep this between us for now," said Ovechkin firmly. He wasn't about to let the base commander's fear put them both in front of a firing squad. He could feel an anxious gnawing in the pit of his own stomach though. Who were those men? Why did they come here? And did they really leave empty handed or were they about to find the President's dead body on the other side of the door?

"Hurry up and get this safe room open. And get a second team working on knocking a hole through the rear wall. We need to get into that room, *now*."

***

"What?" Sokolov demanded of the sergeant standing in his office doorway.

"The Dacha sir, it's gone dark."

"When?"

"Approximately twenty minutes ago, General."

"Twenty minutes?" Sokolov was surprised it had taken this long for anyone to report the problem, "Keep trying to raise them. And get me a helicopter, I need to get to Dolgiye Borody *immediately*."

***

A few minutes later Ovechkin realised his anxiety was perfectly justified. A soldier had come running into the Dacha and saluted the base chief, "The only vehicle to have left the base in the last two hours was a Tigr."

"Someone stole a Tigr?"

"I don't know if it was stolen sir," the soldier confirmed, "but it left base nearly 40 minutes ago, driven by an SPB team."

"An SPB team?" demanded Ovechkin.

"Yes sir," the soldier nodded again, "they had their papers checked at the main gate. Everything was in order. And there is one sentry we cannot account for."

Ovechkin swore loudly. "Circulate details of the vehicle, our missing man and the team to police and army units in the area. Call up the air force if you have to. Authorise and and all necessary force required to stop them."

"We have no comms, sir," Pushkin whispered.

"Take a car into the village. Or a helicopter. Use the damn radio *in* the helicopter. I don't care *how* you do it, just get it done."

"Yes, sir," Pushkin moved quickly down the hallway towards the entrance to the Dacha, collecting the still-dazed sentry along the way, "You're with me soldier."

"Pushkin," Ovechkin yelled over the noise of sawing and demolition, "Tell them to focus on roads heading west. These Poles will be heading for the nearest border."

He turned back to the base chief, "Have me managed to pull CCTV images of the intruders? Do we have a description."

"*Nyet* General," the man shook his head, "They destroyed our IT systems too. It will take some time to recover images from the hard drives. *If* we can get anything back from the disks."

Ovechkin swore again. All he knew for sure was that there were at least four men wearing SPB uniforms, carrying Russian weapons and driving a stolen Tigr.

He was *screwed*.

***

The first they knew of the cellular phone network coming back online was when Ovechkin's mobile began to ring. He almost didn't hear it over the sound of angle grinders, sledgehammer blows and extremely loud cursing from the engineers as they tried to break through the safe room door.

"Yes?" he said, half expecting the call to be from his wife.

"Ovechkin sir? It's Pushkin."

"Yes, Pushkin. Please tell me you have news."

"Yes sir, I do. The Tigr was spotted heading north on the highway where it joined a convoy of other army vehicles being redeployed to the border past St Petersburg."

"And where is the Tigr now?" For the first time in hours Ovechkin felt like his luck was beginning to turn.

"We think it is travelling with the convoy sir."

He watched yet another spray of molten orange sparks arc across Leontin's sitting room as the engineers attacked a recessed door hinge with an angle grinder. *Those sneaky Polish bastards*, he thought. *Nice try, but this ends now.*

"Call the airbase at Ostrov. Tell them to put a pair of attack helicopters in the air immediately."

"But sir…"

"But sir nothing. Do it under my authorisation. And then have the commander call me direct."

"Yes sir."

Ovechkin cut the call and waited impatiently for three minutes until his phone rang again.

"Ovechkin."

"Sir, this is Major Popova at Ostrov. I am preparing two Mi-28 attack helicopters as we speak. Can I ask for what reason?"

"Good day Major Popova," despite the urgency of the situation, the FSO man felt compelled to maintain some semblance of courtesy, "We have a national security issue. A team of foreign agents have infiltrated a column of Russian military vehicles moving north along the M10 highway."

"Yes....?" The Major was hesitant.

"This is a matter of supreme importance," Ovechkin was warming up, "This team is highly skilled and very dangerous. We cannot risk losing them, so you are to eliminate the convoy."

"You mean eliminate the infiltrators?" the Major queried.

"No, you are to destroy the whole convoy. We don't know which vehicle they are in, and we don't have time to find out. This is a matter of national security so, for the security of the Russian Federation, I am ordering you to destroy the convoy with the full authority of the FSO."

There was a shocked silence for a moment, "But sir, this is highly irregular. You want me to attack *our* men?"

"Call me when it is done," Ovechkin hung up, then redialled Pushkin.

"Pushkin, two things. First, contact the convoy leader and get his current location. Second, I want you to call Major Popova at Ostrov and pass on those coordinates. Then get yourself back here to the Dacha."

"Yes sir!"

Chapter Thirty-Nine

Nearly two hours had passed since leaving Dolgiye Borody which meant that the emergency signal should be going out at any moment - assuming it hadn't already. The time had come to leave the convoy and find alternative transport.

"Ease off the power Ksiądz," instructed Wojciech, "Pretend we're having engine trouble and pull over at the service station up there."

Ksiądz began jumping on and off the accelerator, causing the Tigr to lurch back and forward erratically. The truck behind flashed its headlights and the the Priest began coasting slowly into the carpark. He threw his hands comically in the air and shrugged at the driver of the truck behind.

Pulling the Tigr to a stop, he jumped out and opened the bonnet as if to investigate an engine issue. Wojciech waved the rest of the convoy onwards and watched them disappearing into the distance. He was just about to turn away when he spotted two helicopters streaking in low and fast from the west. As he watched they broke formation, one heading south and the other north, performing a sharp turn and gaining altitude until they were facing each other, noses tilted towards the ground.

"Are they in attack formation?" Paweł said from

somewhere behind him.

A sudden streak of light followed by two large explosions and a pall of black smoke were confirmation enough. The two helicopters continued firing rockets until almost a dozen columns of black smoke could be seen rising from the highway ahead.

"Did they just attack and destroy the army convoy?" Ksiądz asked.

"But why? Have we just walked into a civil war?" Paweł followed up.

"I think the security services may have traced the missing Tigr," answered Wojciech, "Either they don't know we have the President - or they don't care."

"Let's hope it's a 'don't know' then," said Ksiądz grinning grimly.

"The trouble is, they know roughly where we are now. And when the security services come to investigate the wreckage, they'll realise they didn't get the right Tigr. I reckon we've got about thirty minutes until that happens."

"So what's the plan, chief?" Ksiądz was still grinning.

"Nothing good, I'm afraid," said Wojciech.

***

Five minutes later, Paweł and Tomasz were back in the Tigr heading towards Pskov and the Estonian border.

"Just 320 kilometres to go," said Tomasz with a wry smile.

"And that's just what the Russians will think," replied Paweł, "I hope."

Tomasz put his foot down and the speedometer needle surged towards the 120km mark. They needed to put as much distance between themselves and the rest of the team as possible.

***

Ovechkin's phone rang insistently. News of the strike on the convoy had obviously reached General Chernov in Moscow. He declined the call.

Chapter Forty

Now in charge of the satphone, Wojciech called Warsaw himself to provide a brief status update and confirm the team had lost two men - or would do very soon. He outlined the situation and could hear the elation sucked from the control room as reality came crashing in like an uninvited guest who treads rancid dog crap into new carpet. With nothing to add, Grabowski had ordered another status update call in two hours time. As in Warsaw, a gloomy silence hung over the vehicle as each man absorbed what had happened to their two comrades.

Wojciech looked out the window of the minivan that Ksiądz had acquired, staring as they passed the burned out shells of the army convoy. The charred remains of dead soldiers could be seen amidst the wreckage, skulls grinning facelessly from the blackened and smoking wreckage. It didn't look like anyone had survived. He could also see police crawling around the burned out shells, trying to identify the vehicles and confirm the presence of the missing Tigr. It was like being back in Kandahar, the acrid smell of burnt flesh fused to mangled metal a stark reminder of their many close encounters with Taliban IEDs. Enemy combatants or not, each one of the dead belonged to, was important to, someone. Wojciech felt the bile rise in his throat and coughed to clear it, to regain his focus.

As Ksiądz accelerated past the shell of the convoy lead vehicle, Wojciech glanced at the prisoner who was lying on the floor of the van. He felt a burning in his chest, rage at the thousands of lives lost because of the maniac at his feet. The pressure increased, building to become an indescribable fury that he was about to sacrifice two of his own men, his friends, for this coward.

"All this just so you could start a pretend war with the US? All this death was worth it?" He yelled at Leontin, "Throwing your own men, your comrades into the slaughter? Now your army is attacking itself, your young men are dying because two old men want to play Cold War 2?"

The President made no effort to speak through his gag. Instead he fixed Wojciech with his own steely glare of unconfined rage. Wojciech resisted the urge to kick the man, turning instead to Ksiądz, "Keep heading north, as quickly as possible."

"Sure thing chief," the driver replied, putting his foot down and quickly pushing through 160km, "We should be in Saint Petersburg in just over an hour."

***

Ovechkin was still pacing in the hallway waiting for one of the two engineering teams to successfully breach the safe room at the dacha. He was also studiously ignoring calls and texts from Chernov. Pushkin was coming along the passageway ending a call on his mobile phone.

Skipping a greeting, the junior man launched straight in with his news, "They missed the Tigr sir. It was definitely not in the wreckage of the convoy."

"The helicopters failed to hit it?" Ovechkin was incredulous.

"No sir, they destroyed every vehicle in the column, every man aboard has been confirmed dead. The stolen Tigr must have separated from the group before the helicopters arrived."

Ovechkin swore loudly, "Tell Major Popova to get his helicopters back in the air. I want them covering the roads towards Pskov. These bastards and their Tigr are heading for the border and they must be stopped."

"Yes sir. Also, we have found the missing sentry. He was shot twice with a large caliber rifle and his body placed in a storage cupboard in the main hall."

"No one thought to search the Dacha?," Ovechkin was livid, "What kind of idiots are running this secure compound?"

***

Paweł felt the helicopter before he saw it, the large rotors allowing it to travel at more than 300 kilometres an hour, just 30 metres above the ground. It thrashed past the Tigr in a blur before pulling up, increasing altitude to assume an attack position.

"I guess this is it," said Tomasz.

"Yes this is it alright," agreed Paweł grinning, "It's time to try out Gennady's special gift."

He pulled a long, green tube out of his pack, opened the ceiling hatch just behind the passenger seat and pushed his head and shoulders through. The oncoming wind tugged at Paweł's cropped hair and he took a moment, eyes closed, to enjoy the rush of air against his skin. Above them, the helicopter had reached the peak of its climb and was beginning to turn, nose angled downwards, pointing at the Tigr.

"Have some of this!" Paweł yelled, pointing the tube skywards and pulling the trigger. There was an enormous *whoosh* as his shoulder-launched Verba surface-to-air missile took flight, streaking towards the attack helicopter ahead and leaving a trail of fire in its wake. The pilot must have seen the rocket because he began to bank away steeply, but it was already too late - the missile had locked-on and found its target with ease. There was an explosion as the warhead detonated and the helicopter collapsed inwards, like a giant fist had punched the fuselage. The flaming wreckage spun and fell, creating a large fireball in the field somewhere behind the speeding Tigr.

Tomasz laughed, a combination of adrenaline and surprise as Paweł climbed back into the passenger seat. He tossed the spent Verba lunch tube into the empty space at the back of the Tigr.

"It's a pity Gennady only gave us one," said Paweł, tears of laughter rolling down his face.

"Why?" asked Tomasz.

"Because I might have been able to take out the other helicopter following us too," he said as a rocket tore through the back of their Tigr, flipping the vehicle into a flaming cartwheel, tumbling end over end along the road.

Chapter Forty-One

A loud crash was accompanied by a weak cheer as the wall-breaching team of engineers beat the door-cutting crew into the safe room. One of the soldiers climbed through the dusty hole, and began helping those trapped inside back out into the light. A man in a black suit with a bloodied nose led the way, followed by an elderly white-haired man, mumbling incoherently. Emerging blinking into the light, Ovechkin was stunned to realise it was none other than Joe Blyden, President of the United States of America - and one of his nation's biggest enemies. Last out was the engineer leading a Russian sentry.

The man in the black suit was a ball of energy, fussing over Blyden, always ensuring he was stood between the him and the Russians assembled in the room. The President himself seemed to be dazed and confused, almost as though he had no idea where he was. He patted at his dust covered suit, murmuring to himself, pausing every now and then to stare mournfully at his secret service minder as if seeking direction on what he should be doing or saying. He looked like a rabbit caught in the headlights of oncoming traffic.

"Is there a reason why President Leontin remains in the safe room?" Ovechkin demanded.

"He's not here sir. They took him," the sentry said, shaking his head. Sensing something very bad was about to happen, the extraction team left their tools and melted quietly into the corridor.

"Who took him? The Poles? Wagner? Or is this an American trick?" The FSO man suddenly realised the situation was far, far worse than he had imagined.

"Poles? These men spoke Russian and were wearing SPB uniforms. We thought maybe it was a coup, that General Chernov was seizing power. Or possibly Wagner."

Ovechkin snorted. Chernov was cunning as a fox, but he lacked the ambition or balls to seize Russia. And as for Prigozhin, the head of the Wagner Group, he was in hiding on borrowed time since his failed march on Moscow.

He turned to Blyden, "Mr President, I do not know why you are here, nor do I wish to. I strongly suggest that you leave Russian Federation territory immediately. I have already lost one President and I have no intention of being blamed for another."

Blyden stared blankly at Ovechkin as though he hadn't understood a single word, his own lips working soundlessly. Perhaps he was in shock or having a traumatic breakdown of some kind.

After a few moments, the black suited secret service man gripped Blyden's elbow gently and shouldered angrily past Ovechkin. The American shot a furious look at the FSO man then began steering Blyden slowly and unsteadily up the corridor towards the main entrance and the SUVs which would take him back to the helicopter waiting on the landing pad a kilometre or so north. The base commander followed them out, trying to distance himself from the wreckage of the safe room, hoping he could find some way to absolve himself of any blame for the disappearance of President Leontin.

"What is going on?" Pushkin whispered as they watched the retreating backs of the men move up the hallway.

"I have no idea," Ovechkin replied, "But you need to get Major Popova back on the phone and countermand the order to destroy the Tigr. Otherwise, we might save the Poles a job and kill the President ourselves."

Pushkin dialled frantically while Ovechkin weighed his options. Chernov was calling again, so he answered with a sigh.

Rather than listen to the General ranting, Ovechkin launched his own counter-offensive, hoping to catch the man off-balance. "I was right sir, the Poles *were* planning something," he began, "However, due to a lack of support and resources we were unable to locate them in time."

"Are you trying to blame me…" Chernov began to say.

"They have been and gone. And now the President is missing, presumed kidnapped. Or worse."

Chernov fell silent.

"Did you hear me sir? I said the President has been taken." Ovechkin could hear the mental wheels turning as his boss considered the implications, or more importantly, how he would be implicated in this disaster.

"So you ordered an airstrike on an army convoy to make sure the President was dead?" the General asked, clearly not planning to accept any of the blame for his subordinate's decisions.

Pushkin was waving at Ovechkin, trying to get his attention, "Sir, I need to call you back." He cut the call without waiting for a response from his superior.

"Popov confirmed they located the Tigr on the road to Pskov as you predicted. Those Polish bastards managed to shoot down an Mi-28 but were then destroyed by the second helicopter in the attack group."

"The Tigr was destroyed? Any survivors?"

"No sir, no survivors. The pilot made a couple of passes of the wreckage to make sure."

"Pushkin," he said wearily, rubbing his eyes, "I think we just killed the President."

Chapter Forty-Two

Standing in the Dacha's entrance, Ovechkin watched with some relief as the US President's Black Hawk helicopter rose just above the trees and accelerated low across Lake Valdai, heading east towards Latvia. The pilot was hugging the ground, avoiding radar contact to ensure their incursion into Russian airspace was not detected. No doubt the legendary Air Force One would be sat at one of the old Russian air bases that dotted the Latvian countryside, waiting to take Blyden the rest of the way home.

If Leontin really was dead, then Russia was about to enter a period of significant political turmoil - and he had helped engineer the disaster. He wondered if Blyden had figured out what had happened, that the Poles had ignored official warnings from their NATO partners. Maybe they would assume it was an internal power struggle, a coup of some kind. Either way, the US could not yet know that Leontin was probably dead.

He stared at Blyden's rapidly retreating helicopter, now little more than a speck on the horizon. The Poles had been exceptionally brave and their plan had almost worked. Given the efforts made to remain undetected on their journey north to the Dacha, would they really have blown their cover at the final stage? He had no doubt that they were headed for the nearest border, but in a vehicle as conspicuous as a Tigr? Army vehicles aren't rare on Russian roads, but they are easy to identify which was why the helicopters had found the escaping Poles so quickly.

He stroked the day-old stubble on his chin thoughtfully and stared at the empty sky above the lake.

***

The pilot of the Black Hawk was fully occupied with keeping the aircraft close to the ground below radar. The route back to friendly airspace had to avoid towns and villages, so he banked and skimmed between forests and fields, travelling as fast and as low as possible. He prayed that the Russians would be true to their word, that any nearby surface-to-air missiles would ignore the helicopter as it passed.

Meanwhile his copilot radioed the waiting Air Force One to confirm he had the president onboard. There was an audible sigh of relief, Blyden's meeting had overrun by some hours. He was so late that some members of his team thought that he may have been kidnapped by an increasingly unhinged Leontin. They had even begun trying to plan scenarios for negotiating his release or perhaps even sending an extraction team, anything to minimise the fall-out from the type of international incident which trigger global conflicts.

Blyden asked for the pilot to activate his personal encrypted circuit, then spoke directly to his chief of staff, "Jeff, we have a problem…"

***

The traffic near Saint Petersburg was heavy, slowing progress of the VW minivan. Surrounded by cars on all sides, Wojciech felt trapped, like they would be discovered at any moment. They were less than two hours from the border of Finland, but it felt more like two hundred thousand as they inched around the ring road that skirted the second city.

Seeing that the men were distracted, Leontin wriggled forward and managed to get himself into a kneeling position so that he could see out the window of the vehicle. He bobbed up and down for a few seconds, hoping that his odd jerky movements would catch someone's attention.

"Uh uh Vlad," said Adam, shaking his head and pushing the President roughly back onto the floor.

"*Kurwa*," said Wojciech, "Was he seen?"

Adam nodded towards the car on their left, "The lady over there in the red Mini is recording us on her cellphone, so I would say yes."

"*Kurwa*," said Ksiądz and Wojciech together.

Adam smiled and gave the Mini driver a conspiratorial wink, "Let's hope she keeps the secret."

Mercifully, the traffic jam began to ease and they were able to pick up speed again. "Good news guys," said Ksiądz forcing himself to feel cheerful, "If we can maintain a decent speed, we should be across the border before dinner time."

"Have you ever tried Finnish food though?" asked Adam with a grimace.

***

Despite the indirect route, the Black Hawk had arrived in Latvian airspace in less than an hour. The helicopter touched down on the crumbling cement apron and Blyden was helped slowly up the stairs to the waiting Air Force One by a waiting aide. The giant blue and white Jumbo Jet was already taxiing towards the runway by the time the President took his seat, muttering and swearing to himself. The four General Electric engines roared with fury, propelling the double-decker plane into the air.

As soon as the fasten seatbelts light was extinguished, Blyden summoned Jeff Zientko, his chief of staff to his office. The man had barely got through the door before President Joe erupted.

"Those disobedient Polish bastards. They were there at the Dacha. They took Leontin."

"They did what?" Zientko asked in disbelief.

"A group of Polish soldiers broke into the Russian compound and kidnapped Leontin. I've been locked in a goddamned closet for the past few hours."

"How much do they know?"

"Enough to sink us. They know I wasn't there to negotiate a ceasefire."

Zientko sighed and looked out the nearest window, wondering what his boss had said, "Did the Russians capture them?"

"I doubt it, no. Leontin and the team were long gone before anyone could release us from the safe room," Blyden seemed most upset by the disrespect of the whole incident rather than the potential criminality, "What do we do now?"

"We make sure they don't get out of Russia, that's what. I'll speak to Lloyd over at Defense, have his intelligence teams track Russian activity near the Dacha and beyond - we can steer him in the right direction to get the job done."

Chapter Forty-Three

With nothing left to do at the Dacha, Ovechkin had been preparing to fly back to Moscow to learn of his fate when Pushkin met him in the main entrance hall, "It's probably nothing sir, but something strange just popped up on Vkontakte."

"More American or Ukrainian fake news no doubt," Ovechkin sighed. Russia's enemies had long used their largest social network as a tool to circulate anti-Leontin propaganda and foment unrest and discord within the Federation. Such was war in the Internet age. "So what have you got?"

"A woman stuck in traffic outside Saint Petersburg says she saw President Leontin in another vehicle. Claims he's on a secret visit to the city."

"Of course she did," said Ovechkin sarcastically.

"I thought the same," Pushkin nodded, "But then I watched the video she shared."

He handed his phone to Ovechkin, a short clip, no more than five seconds long looped on screen. It seemed to show a man's head bobbing erratically around in a car, and then disappearing below the window sill. Ovechkin pinched the screen to zoom in and watched again as the man bounced crazily before a hand reached out from the edge of the frame and gave him a shove, causing the head to disappear. He pinched again, zooming in as close as he could to focus on the face, distorted and grainy, partially obscured by reflections on the glass of the windows. He had to admit, it *did* look a bit like Leontin.

"This is bullshit," he said to Pushkin, "An AI deepfake or something. But we better check it out anyway. Trace the woman and speak to her. See if you can get a description of the car he was in and circulate it to Saint Petersburg police."

Was it possible the Poles had tricked him again? He pulled out his own phone and called Chernov, "We've just had a report that the President is still alive sir. I'm delaying my return while we investigate."

"You're damn right you will Ovechkin," his boss growled, "This entire screw-up is because of you. *You* are going to see this through to the end. Oh, and Sokolov is on his way. Should be with you any moment. Now get the President back."

Ovechkin ended the call and pulled up a map on his phone. If the team had been spotted in Saint Petersburg, they had ignored the shortest, faster, *easiest* routes, which would have taken them to safety in Latvia or Estonia. Which means there had nowhere left to go but Finland, a crazy risk. And with Russian forces already massed on the border to keep those NATO bastards busy, the Poles were trapped. He was confident that the Polish Air Force would not be foolish enough to airlift the men out - all he had to do was get a few units in position to intercept.

He prodded his map again, "Pushkin, contact the Agalatovo base and tell them to mobilise some units immediately. We need them on the road and in pursuit *now*."

While Pushkin placed a call to Agalatovo, he made his own to the commander in Kamenka, asking him to be on standby if required. They no longer had to capture the Polish team, they just had to push them towards the border so there was no room left to manoeuvre. Starve them of choices and they would steer themselves into the trap. For whatever reason, Poland wanted Leontin alive, and Ovechkin was confident the remains of the team would surrender rather than execute him.

He walked towards the front of the Dacha again to await Sokolov's helicopter.

***

A young woman was speaking via secure video link to Zientko, now travelling high above the Baltic Sea, speeding west, "We're seeing increased activity in the regions surrounding Saint Petersburg, sir. Several units have been mobilised in a pincer movement north of the city. They seem to be heading towards the border with Finland at speed."

"Is it an exercise or something more?"

"We're not sure yet sir, but recent activity would suggest they will not cross the border."

"Very helpful, thank you soldier. Please make sure the Department of Defense is informed - and our NATO partners."

"Already on it sir. A NATO rapid response unit is shadowing their moves on our side of the fence."

Zientko nodded and terminated the call. The President had been clear; if the Poles did make it to the border, they were not to cross it. With both sides of the fence strengthened and no way thorough, he just had to sit and wait for the team to give themselves up.

Hopefully Air Force One would be back in Washington by then, well away from this shit show.

***

In Moscow, Chernov was yelling at his secretary, "Get me the Polish ambassador. I want him in my office within the hour."

***

Ksiądz was pushing the minivan as hard as he could, making good time when the satphone rang.

"Quick update," said Grabowski, "We're getting a lot of army radio chatter about the hunt for a small van north of Saint Petersburg. They are mobilising units from the army headquarters at Agalatovo. Orders are to not engage for now, so it sounds like they know who your asset is - and where you are."

"Does that protect us, or make us more of a target?" Asked Wojciech.

"Hard to tell," said Grabowski, "But there's something else. Satellite images show forces lining up on the Finnish border too."

"I guess that's to be expected. A secondary perimeter just in case we make it past the mobile units. It's what I would…"

"*Nie*," Grabowski cut him off, "It's *NATO* forces on the *Finnish* side."

There was a pause.

"Are they preparing to cover us so we can cross the border?"

"*Nie.*"

Another pause.

"We're going to keep heading north. Maybe a gap will open up."

"Very good *kapitan*. Over and out."

Back in Warsaw, Grabowski shook his head. The mission was over and his men were lost. Wojciech was simply delaying the inevitable.

***

Sokolov wasted no time, bawling at Ovechkin for his incompetence, "You fool! You lost the President because you wanted to be the hero."

Ovechkin held his hands out making gentle calming motions in the hope of diffusing the situation, "Alexey my friend, I did not know what the Poles had planned. And I certainly didn't know what *you* had planned,"

"So where is he? Where is Leontin?" Sokolov was not to be pacified.

"You are late," said Ovechkin with a sigh, "The President is in a van somewhere north of Saint Petersburg, heading for the border with Finland."

Sokolov began to interrupt, but Ovechkin continued, "I have mobilised units from Aglatovo and Kamenka to close the border and surround the Polish team. They have nowhere left to go. We can expect their surrender in the next hour or so."

Sokolov stared hard at Ovechkin, "You're done, Yuri. Even if we get him back, you're done."

"And whose job is it to protect the President, Alexey? Specifically?" Ovechkin returned the stare, before breaking into a sly grin, "Now will you wait for the good news here, or do you want to be on the ground when the army captures the Poles?"

Sokolov paled, "Damn you Yuri. Damn you to Hell."

Ovechkin didn't wait. He hurried to the Dacha door loudly demanding that someone drive him back to his waiting helicopter. Pushkin and Sokolov looked at each other for a moment, then scurried after him.

Chapter Forty-Four

"They're screwed. There's nowhere left to run. It's over," Błaszyk slammed his fist into the desk.

One of the other satellite feeds being projected on the wall showed a much wider angle of the Finnish border. Several Russian army units were pushing inwards from the border with Finland. At the same time, NATO units led by US forces were lined up on the other side of the line, creating an impenetrable double wall that ensured no one would escape that way. In the other direction, another column of vehicles and troops was racing up the highway from Vyborg. Wojciech would be able to see them at any moment - assuming he didn't already know that the game was over. Grabowski pulled at his three-day old stubble in frustration.

"He must have spotted them sir, he hesitated for a moment and then turned south," called the operator.

"There's nowhere left to run. Does he think he can swim across the Gulf of Finland?" asked Błaszyk.

"He'll keep running until he's dead sir," Grabowski sighed, "that's the sort of soldier he is. The sort of soldier *you* needed attempt an impossible mission. That's why we chose him."

The group sat in horrified silence, watching the gap

close between the three dots and their pursuers.

"I need to let the President know that it's over," said Błaszyk, heading for the exit.

"No need, Mariusz, I'm already here," said Dudka as he came through the door.

Attention shifted back to the screen. There was a horrified fascination knowing that the last of the team would be dead in a matter of minutes.

***

Following Wojciech's instructions, Ksiądz had left the highway heading south and was now pushing the minivan as hard and fast as possible down a single lane road heading south.

"There," said Adam, pointing at a sharp bend in the road, "There. Let me out there."

Ksiądz looked at Wojciech. Their leader stared out the windscreen for a second before nodding slightly.

"Really?" Ksiądz asked.

Another tiny nod. Wojciech screeched to a halt, just around the bend. Rifle in hand, Adam leapt out and sprinted towards the tree line without as much as a backward glance.

Wojciech slammed the door behind him, "Go! Go!" He screamed at Ksiądz, as he pulled back onto the road.

***

"Why has he pulled off the highway? Does he think he can make it out by sea?" demanded Błaszyk.

"Perhaps," said Grabowski, "Although I think it unlikely. Maybe he is hoping to find some unmarked hunting tracks that can get them to the border."

The vehicle negotiated a tight bend, appearing to

slow for a moment, then one of the remaining four dots separated from the group.

"Someone has exited the vehicle, sir," called one of the operators, "It's Adam. Looks like he's going to try and slow the pursuers."

"He'll buy them some time, but for what?" asked Błaszyk.

"Wait, what's that?" yelled Grabowski, pointing at a cluster of buildings on the display, "There, further south from their current position."

The road ended at a large industrial site and behind it lay the sea. It didn't look like the kind of place to make a last stand, but then the remains of the team didn't have a lot of choice at this point.

"Apparently it's the Portovaya Landfall Facility sir," the operator called out, "Whatever that is, " he muttered to himself.

"You clever, clever bastard," Grabowski whispered, shaking his head in disbelief. Then speaking to the rest of the room, "Apparently it's *not* all over gentlemen, they have one last roll of the dice. But we are going to have to move very quickly. Get me Gdynia on the phone, *right now*."

Chapter Forty-Five

Once into the trees, Adam threw himself into a small hollow in the ground. He rolled onto his front, extended the bipod legs mounted to the underside of his SVDM rifle and began to run through his range finding routine. Squinting through the powerful sniper optic, he focused on the bend in the road, taking a few deep breaths and trying to steady himself. He watched the trees opposite, noting the slight southerly breeze and made a slight adjustment on his optic to compensate. He pulled the bolt action, chambering the first round.

A moment later and the familiar shape of a Tigr rounded the bend. Adam took aim, drew in a breath and let it out slowly. At the same time he squeezed the trigger. There was an enormous bang, then a fraction of a second later, his round punched a hole through the armoured glass and the driver behind it. Adam watched as the vehicle continued to accelerate across the road. Failing to navigate the bend, the carrier flew off the road and into the trees beyond. There was a loud crash as the vehicle slammed into the unforgiving tree trunks.

Adam had already reloaded and fired at the next Tigr which was following close behind the first. Again, a fist-sized hole appeared in the screen, but this time the vehicle skewed sideways across the road before being hit by two canvas-covered trucks following behind. The road was blocked, which should buy Wojciech a few valuable minutes.

Grinning, Adam racked his next shell, watching through his scope as troops began pouring out of the trucks, scanning the tree line for their ambushers. Moving like a well-oiled machine, the Polish sniper began picking off the soldiers one-by-one, as the startled men ran for cover, firing wildly into the trees on both sides of the road.

More troops began to appear from around the corner on foot, moving carefully between the bushes and trunks. These men were more composed and Adam could see them carefully scanning the forest ahead, watching for the muzzle flash of his rifle. As they pinpointed his position, the return fire became more accurate and Adam had to duck his head as bullets sprayed the trees and earth around him. He replaced his magazine and fired back, but the soldiers had taken the momentary pause to find cover, making them much harder to hit. But he had slowed the pursuers *and* depleted their forces somewhat.

A moment later Adam saw a streak of light exit the trees opposite, but the rocket had already exploded before he could even begin to run.

Chapter Forty-Six

Krzysztof Krajewski, the Republic of Poland ambassador to Russia waited patiently in a small room while a uniformed secretary eyed him suspiciously from behind her computer terminal. Things had been quite unpredictable since the invasion of Ukraine and this was not the first time he had been called to the Kremlin. He prided himself on maintaining a cordial relationship with the Russian government even as his country publicly condemned the war, agitating for harsher action and sanctions against the aggressors. But this was the first time that he had been summoned by the FSO, especially as he rarely had any personal dealings with Leontin.

The door to the inner office opened and the secretary gestured Krajewski to enter. Despite knowing where he was, the ambassador was still shocked to be greeted, alone, by the head of the FSO himself, a large bear-shaped Army General, gold trim shining against his grey uniform. Where was the usual coterie of civil servants and bureaucrats? *This is bad*, he thought.

"Ambassador Krajewski," said the man, rising from behind his desk, "I am General Chernov. I would offer you a seat, but you will not be here for long."

Krajewski tilted his head slightly in puzzlement,

trying to read the situation, "How can I be of assistance, General?"

"Ambassador, I must protest in the strongest possible terms regarding the deployment of Polish troops on sovereign Russian soil. Your government must be aware that this is an act of war, so we demand that you order your soldiers to stand down and surrender with immediate effect. Perhaps then we may prevent this incident escalating any further."

"General, I assure you I have no idea about any Polish troops operating in Russia. Obviously I share your concerns and will raise them personally with Warsaw."

"You can call them on your way to the airport Ambassador Krajewski if you wish. You are now *persona non grata* and must leave Russia immediately. You will be flown to Kaliningrad and transported on to the Polish border where your government can collect you. I assume you have your passport?" The diplomat nodded, "Good. There is a car waiting for us downstairs."

"Us?"

"Us. I will be accompanying you to the airport."

Krajewski turned and left the room, his head spinning. Something was happening behind the scenes. Something big. Security officials summoning ambassadors may indicate a military coup was underway. Someone, somewhere had lost control. Whatever was going on, diplomatic protocol had just gone out the window.

He walked down the stairs and out the front door of the yellow FSO building, followed closely by Chernov. A large black car was waiting at the kerb, an armed guard holding the rear door open. Pulling his cellphone from his pocket, he settled in the back seat and the car accelerated away, leaving the Kremlin and heading north towards Sheremetyevo Airport. He glanced across at Chernov who seemed to be absorbed in a call of his own. He should definitely wait until he was alone before calling Warsaw, but this was an emergency.

Krajewski dialled the Ministry of Foreign Affairs, "Rau? Are we at war with Russia?"

***

A few minutes later and another phone was ringing in Warsaw, this time on Błaszyk's desk. The insistent buzzing jolted the Minister from a much-needed nap. He groaned as he lifted the receiver to his ear, "*Tak?*"

"Mariusz, this is Zbigniew. I have just taken a call from our ambassador in Moscow. Are we at war?"

Błaszyk had not expected to hear from Rau, the Minister of Foreign Affairs. He certainly wasn't in the loop for the Leontin mission, "Are we *what?*"

"Krajewski, our ambassador to Russia has been expelled, he's just been loaded onto a plane into Moscow bound for Kaliningrad. The Russians claim there has been an incursion of sovereign Russian territory, that a team of Polish soldiers is operating inside their borders and the Kremlin is demanding our troops surrender immediately."

"That is preposterous," Błaszyk went on the offensive, "There are no Polish troops in Russia. There have never been any Polish troops in Russia. Has Leontin lost his mind?"

"Our ambassador was expelled by a soldier, General Chernov who heads up the Federal Protective Service for Leontin. Apparently this Chernov was quite keen to warn of potential war if our troops do not hand themselves in *right now*."

"I can assure you Zbigniew that there are no Polish troops in Russia, nor are we at war." At least he wasn't lying.

"Those Russian bastards have lost their minds," said a relieved Rau, "I expect we will have to close our Moscow mission entirely now."

"To be honest Zbiegniew, I have much bigger problems to deal with than insane Russian generals right now," Błaszyk said with a sigh, "Now if there's nothing else…?"

"No, that's all. *Dziękuję*"

Błaszyk slammed the phone down on his desk. *How did they….?* With no chance of going back to sleep, he grabbed his jacket and headed back to Mission Control to check the progress of the team.

***

Chernov settled back in his seat as the small executive jet took off from Sheremetyevo just behind Krajewski's. But where the plane bearing the Pole banked west, his own continued in a northerly direction towards St Petersburg and beyond.

The earlier call from Ovechkin worried him. Wasting FSO time and resources chasing foreign spies was one thing. Perhaps the mass disruption caused by the roadblocks in Tver could be explained away too. But launching an airstrike on a friendly army unit? Chernov had given the over enthusiastic academic too much rope - and now Ovechkin was about to hang them both.

Chernov was flying to Pribylovo, a small base just

south of Vyborg where he could transfer to a fast helicopter the moment his two errant subordinates were found. The sooner he located them, the sooner he could shut them down and bring the situation back under control.

Ignoring the prominent no smoking signs the Director of the Federal Protective Service lit a Jin Ling cigarette, enjoying the sharp rasp of the carcinogens as he drew the harsh smoke into his lungs. How had he let Ovechkin spiral so far out of control? And what was Sokolov playing at? Why had his impeccable foreign intelligence sources not picked up the threat to the President? He drummed his fingers absentmindedly, smoking and thinking as the jet streaked towards the Karelian Isthmus.

Chapter Forty-Seven

A large gate blocked the end of the road but Ksiądz didn't slow, hitting it at 90. The metal groaned and buckled inwards but the hinges held firm, throwing the three remaining occupants against their seatbelts, airbags exploding, crushing the air from their lungs. As if in sympathy, the van's engine choked, coughed and died. For a minute or two there was dazed silence. Both airbags had triggered and the air was thick with the dust they released.

Ksiądz turned the ignition key, the engine making a pathetic whining sound but refused to start. He clicked it a few times then shook his head, "It's dead *kapitan.*"

Wojciech nodded his acknowledgement, then slid open the side door and pushed Leontin out in front of him. Wojciech removed the gag from the President's mouth, "If we're going to run, you're going to need to breathe."

"You stupid Polish bastards…"

The gate to the compound had bent and warped, creating a gap through which Ksiądz squeezed his tubby body. Wojciech shoved Leontin head down into the breach and the Priest pulled him through on the other side. Turning his aching head to fit through the mangled bars, Wojciech could hear the sound of many approaching vehicles, a small plume of black smoke curling out of the trees which hid the access road behind them. He tried not to think of what that meant for Adam.

"Now *move*," he said, taking one of the prisoner's arms. Ksiądz grabbed the other and they began half-jogging, half dragging Leontin into the compound past small buildings and assorted pipes and industrial valves. Crashing and stumbling, exhausted and breathless, the men were running on adrenaline alone. Wheezing and ashen, Leontin fell to his knees.

"Stop. We must stop," he panted, staring imploringly at his captors.

Ksiądz snatched a handful of his suit jacket, yanking him back to his feet and propelling him forwards with a shove in the small of his back. With every step they took, the sound of their pursuers got louder. They were out of time.

Rounding a small bend in the road they could see a group of hard-hatted men clustered around some much larger pipes a few hundred metres ahead. They appeared to be craning a large cylindrical object into an open hatch a few metres above the ground.

"There. Head for those men."

They continued to jog but as the paved road gave way to rutted earthen track, Leontin began dragging his feet and stumbling. His fine leather shoes weren't made for running and he was tiring, slowing them down, allowing their pursuers to draw ever closer.

"Run, you bastard, *RUN!*" Wojciech yelled at the man as they inched closer to the group of workers. Distracted by the commotion, the workers were surprised to see two soldiers and a civilian stumbling towards them, assault rifles pointed in their direction. They raised their hands in the universal sign of surrender as the trio stumbled breathlessly towards them.

"Is it live? Is the pipeline filled and pressurised yet?" Wojciech demanded of the man at the front of the group. He gestured with the barrel of his assault rifle, one hand still supporting the exhausted Leontin.

"*Nyet*, we are still preparing. The pipe is fixed and running at minimal pressure but now we test and clean," the man pointed at the long, cylindrical object they were attempting to manoeuvre into the pipe hatch. A series of fan-shaped brushes and rubber fins bristled along each section of the device, interspersed by spring-mounted wheels that pressed against the walls of the pipe. "That's a pig. It scrapes filth and other junk that may have become trapped in the pipeline after it was blown up. Pig also checks the pipe wall integrity to ensure repairs were successful. No leaks."

"Where does it come out?"

"Lubmin. All the way from here to Germany, no stops."

"We're going in, us and him," Wojciech said jerking his thumb at Leontin, "Strap him to the back and get this thing loaded. *Quickly*."

"You're going to take the President to Germany. Through the pipe?"

"We're going to try," said Ksiądz gesturing with his pistol, "and you're not going to stop us."

"Stop you? Us? *Nyet*. You take the bastard," he spat at Leontin. He began yelling instructions to the rest of the team. Two men man-handled Leontin into a harness, while another pair hurriedly unloaded various electrical items from a trolley. The main pig unit was gently levered into the mouth of the pipe and the team tethered the trolley behind it.

"Get on it and lie down," the engineer instructed Leontin. The President stared defiantly at the man for a moment and then did as he was told. A yellow hard hat was slapped, hard, onto his head, while two men strapped Leontin's harness to the trolley so he couldn't fall off.

"You stupid Polish bastards..." he began again before being cut off as the engineers pushed the trolley into the pipe behind the pig.

"Has anyone ever done this before?" Asked Wojciech.

"*Nyet*, but..." the man paused, "Hmmm. But we have sent this equipment through the pipe many times. Maybe your plan will work. You can let me know."

He laughed, handed Wojciech a pair of bright orange rubber ear plugs and slapped him on the back, "Now you on this trolley please."

A volley of small arms fire ricocheted off the pipework around them, announcing the arrival of their pursuers. Ducking low, the pipeline engineers checked the pig's batteries and trolleys one final time, then scattered, running for cover.

"I'll hold them for a few minutes sir," said Ksiądz, "You get after the asset now and I'll follow when I can."

It was hopeless. Facing this many hostiles, Ksiądz wouldn't last more than a few minutes and they both knew it. "It's been a pleasure serving with you *panie kapitanie*," he continued, snapping off a smart two-fingered salute,

"Now if you wouldn't mind hurrying up, I have some Russian soldiers to kill."

Wojciech dropped his rucksack and webbing belt, handing his rifle to his comrade before returning the salute. Then he jumped into the mouth of the pipe before Ksiądz could see his tears.

"Wait!" Wojciech could feel cold water being splashed over him as the Priest performed a final holy water blessing, "Be blessed my son!"

"*Dziękuję* Ksiądz my friend," he called as the pipeline hatch closed and darkness swallowed him, "*dziękuję.*"

The entry hatch slammed closed and the pig began to pull away.

***

"Sir, we've lost kapitan Wojciech and Leontin," one of the young operators called over the top of her computer screen.

Sure enough, there was now just one red beacon, Ksiądz, showing on the satellite overlay.

"Because there's no satellite reception under water soldier," Grabowski explained tersely. At least, he hoped that was why the yellow dot had disappeared.

***

"They are in the pipeline sir," reported the unit commander, "What do you want us to do?" Ovechkin could hear the rattle of automatic rifles over the noise of his helicopter's rotors.

"They *what*?" he yelled.

"Two of the targets have gone into the pipeline. Repeat, two men in the pipe.," the commander repeated himself twice, trying to convince himself as much as

Ovechkin, "And we have a small number of hostiles providing covering fire for their escape."

"Neutralise the defence then, you fool," screamed Ovechkin, trying to buy some time.

"But what about the men in the pipe?"

"Get the scene under control. Do whatever needs to be done. *Use your damn initiative.* We will be with you in five minutes."

"Very good sir," the commander cut the call.

As the helicopter pilot circled looking for place to land, Ovechkin examined the Nordstream Landfall facility below. A bewildering array of pipes and valves and hatches glinted in the sun as they ran in two lines towards the sea. Looking back inland he could see a collection of military vehicles, surrounded by a swarm of soldiers in fatigues. They were all shooting towards a truck, about 200 metres ahead. From his vantage point in the sky, Ovechkin could see a single man crouched behind the vehicle, providing suppressive cover as a team of engineers scattered for safety at the edge of the compound, away from the battle.

Peering out of his own window, Sokolov was surprised to see one man was holding back a battalion. A small battalion, but a battalion nonetheless. He felt a grudging admiration for the bravery of the Poles - and dismayed by the incompetence of the Russian soldiers.

Ovechkin snatched up his phone again, "You are being made to look a fool by a single man, commander. Finish this. Now."

***

"We need to get our submarine back to the Nordstream pipeline as quickly as possible," said Grabowski.

"Back?" asked Dudka, "I have no idea what you are talking about."

"Yes sir," said Grabowski quietly, "Back."

"I still have no idea what you are talking about General," the President replied, shrugging insincerely.

"Mr President," said Grabowski through gritted teeth, "You and I both know it was a Polish submarine that sabotaged the Nordstream pipeline, but we can also both pretend someone else did it. Either way, we need to get our submarine back out there as quickly as possible. Our men and the Russian President are both in the pipe *right now*. And we need to get them out, *right now*."

Dudka said nothing, stroking his chin for a moment.

"*Right. Now*," Grabowski was practically screaming, "Before it is too late."

Dudka nodded, "Make the call."

Chapter Forty-Eight

The commander on the ground sent two platoons left and another two right, circling around behind the lone gunman ahead. The rest of his troops provided heavy suppressive fire of their own in an effort to keep the Polish fighter distracted. A heavy machine gun mounted on the roof of one of the trucks began raking the area around the hatch, large caliber rounds thudding into the ground, kicking up clods of earth.

Ksiądz fell back towards the pipes where Wojciech had disappeared a few minutes earlier, lead ricocheting off the pipes and hatches that surrounded him. He crouched down and squinted between the towering metalwork towards the Russian trucks clustered in the distance. He saw the two groups of soldiers detach themselves and head out towards his flanks. *Hardly surprising really*, he thought, *it's exactly the same manoeuvre any army in the world would use facing a situation like this.*

He reached into his pack and retrieved four fragmentation grenades, placed there by Gennady just two nights earlier. It wouldn't be enough to stop them all, but it would buy Wojciech some time. In one fluid movement he stood, threw a grenade towards the soldiers moving right and ducked back behind the pipes as a hail of bullets pinged and whizzed around him. There was a loud explosion followed by a brief silence before the air was torn by the sound of injured men howling in pain.

Ksiądz didn't wait. He repeated the move, this time tossing the bomb to his left and another directly towards the trucks and machine gun ahead. Each time the explosion was followed by screams. *That should even things up a bit.*

As the smoke cleared, the Russian commander scanned the carnage through his binoculars. There was blood everywhere and at least ten of his men had been hit by shrapnel, their comrades pulling them backwards, trying to find some cover away from the firing line. He ducked as the Pole resumed firing, bullets bouncing off the armoured trucks around him.

Ksiądz checked his ammunition, even with Wojciech's gear he had just one magazine remaining. He pushed it home and chambered the first shell. Peering through the gaps in the pipework, he methodically scanned the area for movement. Each time he saw feet or a face, he fired a single shot, surprised by how many hits he managed to make - Adam would have been impressed. His thirty bullets didn't last long, but every second delayed was a second closer to safety for Wojciech. He tossed the rifle aside and unholstered his pistol and firing through his last two clips to buy a little more time.

After a few minutes, the commander realised the firing had stopped because the cries of the injured and dying were even louder now. He sent the order to his men to move in *carefully*, the hostile appeared to have finally run out of ammo.

The Russians surrounded Ksiądz and he emerged

from behind the pipes, hands held high and a wide grin on his face.

"*Privet!*" He greeted them waving and striding confidently into the group of waiting soldiers, muttering, "Greater love hath no man than this."

Before anyone could stop him, Ksiądz had embraced the commander in a bearhug. Only then did they notice the grenade pin hooked on his finger.

***

Control had watched in silence as the Russians cornered Ksiądz. Then there was a collective gasp, as the screen lit up with a brief flash and the soldiers seemed to fly backwards. When the image refocused, they could see bodies of the dead and injured splayed outwards from the upper torsos of Ksiądz and the field commander, still locked together in a fatal embrace. Błaszyk looked like he was about to vomit while Dudka was thankful the satellite feed did not have audio. Grabowski just hoped the Priest had died instantly.

Chapter Forty-Nine

The pig accelerated down a gentle slope, its wheels generating a loud hum that reverberated against the walls of the tunnel. This was joined by a harsh squealing cause by the fins and brushes scraping the surface of the pipe. Yet the increased atmospheric pressure meant that the sound of blood rushing in his own ears was still louder than the industrial noise that surrounded Wojciech. Occasionally he imagined he could hear Leontin cursing or crying, but even with the earplugs, the roaring of the automated pipe cleaner drowned out everything until he could feel it rattling in his bones, vibrating in his teeth.

As time dragged on, the humming and thumping became hypnotic and Wojciech could feel himself slipping into a half-conscious dream where the events of the last week played like a movie in his head. The black car waiting to whisk him away from his wife and the girls. The joy of meeting up with his old JWK team mates. Their lunatic sprint across the Ukrainian frontline and a drive across half of Russia. All moments of dissociated joy or heartbreaking sorrow.

And it got worse when his friends had started to die, sacrificing themselves for the Fatherland. No, not the Fatherland, for the rest of the world. A desire for peace that their 'peace-loving' allies didn't seem to share. In the darkness, his rage flared brightly. The very worst thing that could happen now would be to fail, rendering all their sacrifices meaningless.

He gritted his teeth and settled in for what could be days of hungry darkness until they reached a 'friendly' country. He wondered what the Germans would say when Leontin popped out of their pipeline. And how Grabowski would go about rescuing him.

***

The Polish General was in luck. ORP Orzeł was already back at sea, the kilo-class submarine on a routine NATO patrol of the Gulf of Finland, silently shadowing Baltic Fleet traffic out of Kaliningrad.

"Again?" The submarine's captain asked.

"Yes," said Grabowski, "But it has to be today."

"Where?"

"Wherever they are in the pipe. And so long as it is in international waters."

"They? There's people *in* the pipe?"

"Yes. Two men in the pipe, travelling west. We need you to get them out."

The commander swore under his breath, "Very good sir."

He stared at the radio handset for a moment, then began issuing instructions. "Ensign, activate the acoustic transponder. Tune it to the frequency for the pipeline. Lieutenant, take us down to 100 metres on heading 050, maximum speed. And get the chief engineer to the bridge, I need to know how to get two men out of a pipeline at the bottom of the Baltic sea."

The crew of ORP Orzeł submarine became a blur of activity as each man went to work.

Chapter Fifty

The helicopter had barely touched their ground before Ovechkin had leapt out. He was greeted by a saluting sergeant just outside the reach of the rotors, "We've lost them sir."

"What do you mean, 'lost them'?" Ovechkin was incredulous, "You had them cornered, where could they go?"

"We've lost them," the sergeant repeated himself, "Two men have disappeared into the gas pipeline. They're probably half way to Germany already. The other soldier killed our captain."

"They did *what*?" A cold sweat broke out across Ovechkin's back.

"One man blew himself up. The other two went into the pipeline. The Nordstream engineers say that we have no way to catch them or bring them back. They are gone - and they probably won't survive."

Ovechkin felt his stomach lurch, a liquid churn in his gut. He turned to face the hulking form of Sokolov standing behind him.

"Yuri?"

"You are in charge now Alexey, so you must decide what to do.," the SPB man spoke in a low voice so the sergeant could not hear him, "If the Poles get him out, Russia will be embarrassed - and *we* will be made to pay."

Ovechkin turned away a hand tugging absentmindedly at his wild grey hair. He span back on his heel, a determined, steely look set on his face, "Bring the Nordstream engineer here. Now."

The sergeant signalled to his men clustered around the trucks. Two peeled away from the group, leading a sheepish looking man in blue overalls.

He didn't wait for any introductions, "We need to follow them."

"Follow who?" the engineer asked, playing dumb.

"Don't piss me around, the men in the pipe. We need to follow them *immediately*."

"Alexey, this is madness," Sokolov intervened.

"No Yuri, someone must go after them. *I* must go after them. I must catch them." He was serious.

The engineer stroked his chin and looked at the floor, "We have another pig. It is smaller, lighter and faster so you may catch them in a few hours. Maybe. Or maybe you die too." He shrugged unsympathetically.

"Get it set up. Now."

"It's your funeral," the engineer muttered. He let out a shrill whistle and gestured his colleagues to gather round. He began to issue instructions, men running in different directions to make the necessary precautions.

"Alexey," Sokolov tried again, "You cannot do this, Vladimir is gone. We must think of something else."

"Like blow up the pipe to make sure? No Yuri, I am going after him. I will bring him back."

He turned and strode quickly towards the large

hatch where the engineers were beginning to gather. In the distance a forklift truck exited a small shed at speed, carrying a long cylindrical machine, pulling up next to the workmen who were already loading a trolley into the opening.

"You must go first," the foreman explained, "The pig will push you. If you do catch the others, you will be able to reach them."

"Fine. Now hurry up," he turned to Sokolov, "Yuri, give me a gun."

"Do you even know how to use a gun, Alexey?" the SPB man sighed.

"I can learn."

"You have no time to learn. You will only kill yourself in the dark. Take a knife instead." He reached into his jacket pocket and handed the man a thin, vicious-looking switchblade. Ovechkin examined it for a moment testing the release spring, then put it into his trousers. The engineers rigged a restraining strap and helped him onto the trolley, before lifting it into the mouth of the pipe. Ovechkin slid out of sight as the pig was inserted behind him. The foreman completed one last check and set the machine running, its wheels gripping the pipe walls pushing it forwards into the tube.

***

For Wojciech the darkness was total, except for a regular red flashing light on the pig ahead. Occasionally the pipe turned gently, the red flash illuminating the smooth metal walls. If he tilted his head and arched his back he could see Leontin's shiny black leather shoes illuminated for a fraction of a second, just a few centimetres away from his face. In all the time they had been in the tunnel, the President hadn't moved and Wojciech wondered if the man was actually asleep.

Unable to sit up and with just a few centimetres clearance on each side, there was nowhere to move. Wojciech massaged his thighs, trying to work some feeling back into his legs, numbed by the thrumming vibrations that travelled through his body. It was uncomfortable but he was grateful that there wasn't enough room for Leontin to slide off the trolley - or to attack him. He assumed the Russian must have resigned himself to his fate, otherwise he would surely have tried kicking Wojciech in the face by now.

Mile after mile, the roaring, rumbling pig rattled and hummed westwards, its mechanical brushes sweeping the walls and blowing rust and dust particles into his face. He thought of his comrades and their families, how he would have to break the news of their deaths. How they had willingly sacrificed themselves to change the world. How their families would be devastated. Wojciech felt guilty, sad that he had got lucky, that he would soon see his wife and girls again - and for no other reason than his superior rank.

But it was the thought of his girls that had brought him this far, had made him agree to this crazy, impossible mission. He wanted a world that was safe for them, where they didn't have to worry about a war on their doorstep.

The solid darkness seeped into his soul. He yelled and howled, but the roaring of the pig drowned him out. Finally, overcome by exhaustion, the last of his adrenaline spent, Wojciech passed out, the blackness of the pipe merging with his own.

Chapter Fifty-One

As the senior official on site, Sokolov called an impromptu conference with the Nordstream foreman and the ranking officer from the Army unit.

"Will he catch them? Really?" Sokolov asked the foreman, nodding in the direction of the pipeline

"It will take some hours, but yes, he should do." The man nodded.

"And if he does, will they get out?"

"Like I told the other soldier, maybe. Probably not," the man shrugged, "It's a one-way trip all the way to Germany. It will probably take them a few days to get there, even if we increased the atmospheric pressure inside the pipeline."

A knife-wielding bureaucrat fighting a trained special forces soldier in an enclosed space? Ovechkin was already as good as dead - as was Leontin. But should he let nature take its course, or…?

He turned and pointed at the sergeant, "You. You're in charge now. Blow it."

"What?"

"I'm promoting you. You're in charge of this unit now. Blow up the pipeline."

The soldier completely ignored his spontaneous

increase in rank, "But all three men will die sir."

"*Da*. You said it yourself, they are already gone. Blow the pipeline. Flood it. Now."

"But..." The soldier began.

Sokolov spoke slowly, hoping no one could detect the tremor in his voice, "Blow. The. Pipe. Now."

"Yes sir." The sergeant saluted, turned and began issuing urgent orders to his men.

***

"Slow to 8 knots," Captain Sikora ordered.

"Slowing to 8 knots."

The sound of the transponder ping echoed through the bridge. The Orzeł was cruising alongside the pipeline, keeping pace with the pig inside.

"We're going to set down atop the pipe to create a seal under our lower hatch. Once the seal is in place, one man will enter the hatch and cut through the pipe wall with an acetylene torch to give us access."

"And the pig?"

"We can jam the transponder signal as it passes the hatch. The pig will stop automatically and we can then extract the men behind it."

"Are you sure this will work, Chief?"

"Maybe," the Chief Engineer shrugged, "You get the sub on the pipe *ahead of the pig* and I'll take care of everything else."

***

"The charges are ready sir."

"You're sure the pipe will be completely flooded?"

"Yes sir., my men have laid charges below the waterline. Once detonated, they will take out a significant section of pipe."

"Very good, Captain" Sokolov nodded, "Blow the pipe."

The Captain stared hard at the SPB man for a fraction of a second before repeating the command into his radio, "Go. Repeat, go."

Sokolov turned towards the sea where two enormous gas pipelines sloped down into the water. Moments later there was a loud explosion, water erupting upwards in an enormous fountain of froth, glittering weakly in the sunlight. Even at this distance they could see two large, sucking whirlpools forming as the inky waters of the Baltic rushed to fill the empty Nordstream pipes.

***

For the second time in a matter of minutes, the watchers in Warsaw lost visual contact as the screen flashed out following a large explosion.

"What was that? Did they just blow the pipes?" The Polish President demanded.

"It certainly looked like an explosion," Błaszyk agreed.

Grabowski was silent, of course it had been an explosion. It seemed as though his team was about to snatch defeat from the jaws of victory, unable to complete their second impossible task. The mighty Baltic Sea would rush into the fractured pipes, an unstoppable wave surging through the darkness, taking the last of his men with it. A truly terrible way to die.

"We may not have got Leontin, but he won't be making any trouble for us again," said Dudka, "Not our intended outcome obviously, but I would say the mission was a success. Now call the Orzeł back before she is detected and we start an international incident."

"No," said Grabowski in a whisper.

"No?" The President echoed in surprise.

"No *sir*," Grabowski repeated, slightly louder this time, "The Orzeł will continue on course as planned until we can confirm our man is dead."

"If he's not dead already, he will be dead in a matter of minutes General, so…"

"*No!*" Grabowski yelled.

Chapter Fifty-Two

Wojciech awoke with a jump, banging his helmeted head on the pipe above.

"What is happening Polish? Why are we stopped?" Leontin asked from the darkness somewhere ahead.

He was right, the pig had stopped, the silence and darkness complete. There was no space to move and he had no idea how to restart the pig. The Russians must have terminated it remotely. Wojciech tried not to think of slowly dying in this tiny enclosed space, so far from home. Would they suffocate? Starve? Die of thirst?

"Looks like your countrymen have had enough of you too, eh Vlad?" he taunted.

Wojciech closed his eyes, blinking back tears of exhaustion and despair. His team had come so close to pulling off the impossible and ending a war. And now they were all dead.

Suddenly a blinding shower of sparks sprayed down from the roof of the pipe. A glowing orange line of melted metal appeared, slowly tracing to form a ring.

"What the…?" Leontin was cut off as a section of pipe fell, hitting him in the midriff and momentarily winding him. A shaft of bright light shone from the roof above.

"*Dzień dobry* gentlemen," said a smiling face, poking through the hole.

***

Sokolov watched expectantly as a large attack helicopter streaked fast and low across the surface of the Gulf of Finland heading directly for the Landfall Facility. The aircraft circled once and then set down beside the Mi-8 in which he had arrived thirty minutes earlier.

No sooner had the tricycle undercarriage made contact with the earth then the side door opened and Chernov jumped out, pausing for a moment to scan the area. Spotting Sokolov, the unmistakable bear-shaped man began striding towards his subordinate,. Everything about the man radiated rage and for a moment the SPB man was afraid.

"Where is the President?" Chernov shouted over the whining rotors. With its underwing mounted cannons and rockets, the helicopter looked as dangerous and aggressive as he did.

"It is done, General, he is gone."

"Gone?" Chernov stared hard at Sokolov, "What do you mean 'gone'?"

"I mean that the Poles put him in the Nordstream pipeline," the SPB man explained, "Ovechkin followed, but he will never catch them. He will never bring the President back, Leontin is gone. So I blew the pipe."

"What have you done, Alexey? That's insane."

"I am perfectly sane, Dmitry," Sokolov replied. He was calm, as though a weight had lifted from his shoulders and a smile of relief spread across his face, "I could not have predicted the journey, but it was always going to end this way."

The colour drained from the General's face as the penny dropped, "*Starszy sierżant*, arrest this man!"

The newly promoted soldier was horrified, unable to fully understand what was happening. He looked from man to man, hoping for a clue, something that would tell him what was going on.

"Arrest him now!" Chernov yelled.

With two privates flanking him, the still-smiling Sokolov was marched away to one of the waiting trucks.

***

"Sir, we have a problem," the chief engineer signalled to the Captain.

"What is it?"

"It could be a sensor malfunction, but there seems to be a second transponder coming up fast behind our target."

The Captain swore, "Disable it. Now."

"I'm not sure we can sir, it appears to be using a different transponder frequency."

Chapter Fifty-Three

Wojciech had unstrapped himself from the trolley and struggled forwards to free Leontin. The Russian said nothing, staring hatefully as his captor.

"Come on Vlad, as much as I want to, I can't leave you here," Wojciech said, pushing the Russian towards the hole in the pipe above. At the same time, the sailor was grunting and sweating, trying to grab Leontin under the shoulders and lever him into the waiting submarine.

A sudden blast of air raced through the blackness from the direction they had come, tugging at Wojciech's uniform, causing his scalp to prickle under his short, military haircut. It was followed almost immediately by a low roar that seemed to be rapidly increasing in volume.

"Well Polish," said Leontin, "They have given up on catching you and rescuing me. Now they have decided we must both die."

The President allowed himself to go limp, his deadweight almost impossible to shift.

"What are you talking about?" asked Wojciech, having to raise his voice over the thunder behind them.

"That noise? They have blown up the pipe, Polish," Leontin sighed with a resigned smile, "It is over. Now we both die here in the dark."

There was a splintering crash as something smashed into the trolley, throwing Leontin and Wojciech forwards. The sailor above screamed in agony as the pig shifted, one of its giant wheels rolling over his forearm, shattering the bones. His face disappeared from the hole, but was quickly replaced by another who began frantically tugging at Leontin, hauling him towards the light.

Looking between his feet, Wojciech could see there was something behind them in the pipe, but he couldn't make out any details in the darkness. The shadows moved and reformed, a sliver of silver light arced out of the black and buried itself in his right thigh. It took Wojciech a moment to realise it was a knife, that he had been stabbed, that it bloody hurt.

The blade swung again and again he was too slow, landing even higher on his thigh and causing him to cry out in pain. One of the shadows was slithering towards him, onto him, scrabbling, clawing, slashing, crushing. He swung wildly with his left boot, stamping and hacking, but the man kept coming. The roaring was getting louder too, and as he fought for his life he wondered if it was the sound of his rage and pain manifested.

The blade slashed again and Wojciech was able to grab the hand that held it, slamming the wrist against the pipe wall. *Smack, smack, smack,* the fingers finally released their grip and the switchblade was lost somewhere in the dark. But the man was not done, he was panting and growling and yelling, pummelling Wojciech before reaching for his throat, everything disappearing in a stupendous roar that seemed to fill the entire universe.

And then he was hit by a train, a solid wall of water

slamming into him. Caught unaware, Wojciech swallowed a mouthful of freezing seawater, coughing and choking as the surge rushed past. It tore at his aching, bleeding limbs, crushing him, Leontin and his attacker against the pig. Just as he thought his lungs would burst, the water receded, falling back level with the trolley he lay on. The flood had temporarily incapacitated his attacker, but already he could feel the man beginning to crawl up the pipe, using Wojciech to pull himself towards the circle of light above.

"Take him!" Wojciech yelled, pushing Leontin up through the hatch. There were now two sailors reaching through the gap above, four hands struggling to haul the Russian president through the narrow opening and into the submarine. The initial wave created by the explosion back at the Landfall Facility had passed, but the inky water behind was rising rapidly, the pipe already more than half full. Wojciech could feel the current strengthening, pulling him as his boots slipped on the polished metal walls of the pipe.

He glanced down at the man who was crawling over him, the wild-eyed face just a few inches from his own. Wojciech was surprised to see it was the crazy haired man from the Dacha, mouth moving soundlessly, hands clawing at Leontin, trying to prevent him from being taken.

With one last superhuman effort, Leontin's legs disappeared into the submarine. In his half-sitting, half-lying position, the water was rushing over Wojciech's shoulders and face, forcing itself into his mouth and nose. He coughed and spluttered as hands above and below grasped desperately, clawing at his shoulders, face, hair. One pair willing him into the light, the other pulling him towards eternal darkness. The weight of the desperate Russian was too much for him to shift and there was no room to move. He was pinned to the trolley. "Close the hatch!" he yelled at the men above him, his head dipping under water again, "Close it! Close it now!"

The current was too strong. With a loud sucking noise the water finally loosened the pig's grip on the pipe walls. The device began sliding, past the hatch and the frantic hands of the sailors, pulling Wojciech and Ovechkin in its wake. The waiting men caught a last glimpse of their upturned faces and then they were gone, lost to the dark rushing waters of the Baltic.

Chapter Fifty-Four

The voyage across, under, the Baltic Sea back to Gdynia was conducted in complete silence. Above them, Russian and NATO frigates criss-crossed the waves, playing hide-and-seek with each other in a series of drills designed to intimidate and impress. Pushing, probing and provoking, each ship testing the readiness and capabilities of their opponents. Yet despite the shows of strength, none of them knew that the Russian President was passing beneath their bows - and Commander Sikora wanted to keep it that way.

Friendly and hostile, all of the ships were scanning the waters below with their sonar arrays and Sikora had no doubt they would happily 'accidentally' fire torpedos or anti-submarine rockets at the Orzeł should it be detected. And so his crew worked tirelessly, wordlessly over the next 18 hours to navigate around Estonia, Latvia and Lithuania and past Kaliningrad, home of Russia's Baltic Fleet.

The bulbous, black shadow of the Orzeł slid into berth at Gdynia just before dawn the following day. Leontin was bundled up the ladder to the main hatch and presented to General Grabowski who was waiting on the darkened dock. Now in Poland, the President looked like a broken man, grey and sagging and aged. Almost pitiable. Nothing at all like the shirtless Russian superman so often seen on television. Grabowski felt a swelling sense of pride at a job well done as well as an immense sadness at the human cost.

Eventually he spoke, "Vladimir Vladimirovich Leontin, I am placing you under arrest for the war crime of unlawful deportation of population (children) and that of unlawful transfer of population (children) from occupied areas of Ukraine to the Russian Federation under articles 8(2)(a)(vii) and 8(2)(b)(viii) of the Rome Statute."

The Russian said nothing, a slight shrug the only sign that he had heard and understood. Grabowski stared at Leontin for a moment longer, then nodded to the two soldiers behind him.

They walked Leontin to Grabowski's car for the short drive to Gdynia-Kosakowo airforce base where a waiting Skytruck transport plane would fly him, unannounced, to stand trial for war crimes at the International Criminal Court in The Hague.

"I think you'll want to see this, sir," Commander Sikora said, holding something out to Grabowski. In his hand was a smartphone, wrapped in notepaper and secured with an elastic band. Grabowski raised an eyebrow questioningly.

"We found it in Leontin's pocket. We think your man stuffed it in there as he was being boarded."

"*Dziękuję,*" Grabowski said, saluting.

***

In Russia, Leontin's kidnap had been blamed on rogue Wagner mercenaries angered by the assassination of their leader, Yevgeny Prigozhin. But as the man responsible for protecting the President, Sokolov had to pay. His trial for crimes of treason was held behind closed doors, a mere formality as would have been the case back in the days of the Soviet Union.

After the charges had been read, former Deputy Director Sokolov stood defiantly in front of the judge and delivered a short statement but did little to actually defend himself. He admitted passing secrets to a hostile nation and encouraging them to topple the Russian head of state. He criticised the war in Ukraine, blaming Leontin personally for the death of his only son who had been killed in the early skirmishes of the Battle of Kherson. From that moment he had sought an opportunity to make Leontin pay. So when the president had asked him to prepare a clandestine meeting at the official dacha, he had passed what little he knew to an old contact in Warsaw.

The fact that Leontin had been kidnapped and publicly humiliated by the Poles was a bonus - he had hoped that the Americans send a hit squad. But the new Cold War plan had put paid to that. There was only one aspect of his treachery for which he expressed regret - sanctioning the assassination of his old friend Jankowski. However, he needed to maintain his secret until someone, *anyone*, took the bait and came for Leontin.

Privately, the new regime was relatively sympathetic to the former SPB man, but they couldn't be seen to be weak - or to totally undermine Leontin. Since his arrest, Sokolov had undergone several beatings, including one from Chernov himself. Not because of loyalty to Leontin, or even out of respect for the law, but because he had humiliated his colleagues. He had shared state secrets for decades and no one had even suspected him.

In reality, Sokolov's actions had provided the

excuse Russia needed to negotiate a ceasefire with Ukraine. But with the world trying to understand what had happened and why Federation forces were falling back to their equally disputed 2021 positions, it was imperative that peace was not seen as defeat for Russia.

The judge wasted no time on deliberations, his verdict swift and unsurprising. Sokolov was sentenced to death.

Legal formalities complete, Sokolov was returned to Lefortovo prison. After the routine embarrassment of being stripped and searched, he redressed in his prison uniform. Two guards flanked him as he limped to his cell. None of the men spoke, their footsteps echoing loudly in the featureless, grey corridor. One guard unlocked the cell door and stood aside, allowing the prisoner to enter. Sokolov had made two steps into the room when the second guard drew his pistol and shot him in the back of the head.

***

The air was damp and chilly and a low mist clung to the ground as Grabowski waited patiently at the border between Poland and the Kaliningrad oblast, that strange, disconnected yet vital outpost of the Russian Federation. In the distance, behind the gate on their side of the border, he could see Russian sentries eyeing him nervously like he was about to mount a one-man invasion. On the Polish side, four soldiers were hurriedly rolling back razor wire that had been placed across the road to strengthen the border since it was closed. When the gap in the fence was large enough, Grabowski's truck edged forward slowly into no man's land.

As the rising sun began to gild the leaves of the

surrounding trees he saw an unmarked truck emerge from the Russian side of the border. It drew up alongside the waiting Polish vehicle in the gap between the two countries.

A uniformed soldier wearing the badges of the Russian Logistical Support division jumped down from the cab and lowered the folding flap at the rear of the truck. With the aid of his comrades, he unloaded four plain wooden coffins and silently transferred them to the Polish vehicle. Grabowski held his salute as each body passed before him. Transfer complete, the Russians soldiers offered the General and the coffins a salute of their own, a gesture he found strangely moving.

Satisfied that all was in order, he nodded his appreciation to the Russians before climbing back into the cab to take his men home for the last time.

***

The unexpected appearance of Leontin in The Netherlands created an intense media storm. The International Criminal Court was thrown into disarray. Despite having issued charges against Leontin, no one had expected to see any movement on the case for several years. Most had doubted they would ever see the Russian President in the dock. Confusion about how exactly he had appeared in The Hague even led some to question whether the case could actually go ahead.

As the wheels of justice slowly ground into action, Leontin rediscovered his voice. He continued to protest his innocence and his refusal to acknowledge the legitimacy of the ICC. "Russia is not a signatory of the Rome Statute and therefore the International Criminal Court has no right to detain or prosecute Russian citizens," he growled menacingly during a preliminary hearing.

Initially, Leontin defence was aggressive. He maintained that Russia had taken back Ukraine in line with the citizens' desire to stamp out local nazis and return to their Fatherland. At one point the now-former President claimed that his was a divine mission of liberation, blessed by the Russian Orthodox Church. He also argued that his capture was illegal, that a foreign power had violated the sovereignty of the Russian Federation and that his detention and trial should be ended immediately. Day after day he sat in court looking bored or angry, buoyed by nothing but his ego.

It quickly became clear that the trial could not proceed immediately because the various investigations into his alleged crimes had yet to be completed. It was decided that Leontin would be held on remand at the ICC Detention Centre in Scheveningen Prison until they were.

After some months, and at the prompting of his defence counsel, Leontin began sharing more details about the planned resumption of the Cold War. In the hope of clemency, or simply reducing his sentence, Leontin implicated the Blyden administration, naming the US President as an active supporter of the hostilities in Ukraine.

***

Initially there was worldwide disbelief, particularly as the Blyden family had been so active in Ukrainian business affairs before the Russian invasion. And as a suspected war criminal, Leontin was hardly a credible source. But when a series of photos showing Blyden secretly meeting Leontin in Russia were leaked simultaneously to media outlets and law enforcement agencies across the world, public opinion shifted quickly. Especially when the FBI was able to show that the images were authentic and had not been tampered with in any way.

As public outrage intensified, further investigations by a Senate Oversight Committee discovered evidence of communications between the White House and the Kremlin. Before the first Russian soldier crossed into Ukraine, Washington and Moscow had been trading ideas on how to create a global stand-off and trigger a new arms race. There was even a suggestion that plans for a new Cold War had been underway for many years with some communications implying a previous US administration had encouraged Leontin in his efforts to take Crimea back in 2014.

Now Blyden was facing a perfect political storm - a stagnant economy, falling approval ratings, a rapidly approaching election and little to show for his Green New Deal. Initiating a global arms race could change everything, yielding immediate economic growth and spurring massive investment in military R&D. More importantly still, a wider conflict would trigger new sales to other NATO members. Desperate to shore up his dwindling re-election chances, the President had escalated his clandestine support for an invasion of Ukraine.

Given the weight of evidence against him, Blyden was impeached by Congress and removed from office before Leontin's trial even began. Hoping to avoid further embarrassment and at the urging of his defence team, Blyden was quietly declared unfit to stand trial and pensioned off to a residential care facility.

***

While attention was directed at Leontin's trial and the nomination of Blyden's replacement, Poland remained silent about their role in both. Full details of the exfiltration operation were never published, nor was the team of volunteer soldiers ever publicly identified. Unable to explain exactly how Leontin came to be in The Hague, the world's media assumed it was the result of a Russian power play, an internal coup led by disgruntled oligarchs and ambitious subordinates. As for Poland, attention quickly shifted to the upcoming elections and potential defeat for WiS at the polls.

In Warsaw, a short ceremony was held behind closed doors at the Sejm Chapel in Warsaw for the families of Wojciech, Paweł, Tomasz, Ksiądz and Adam. President Dudka himself gave a short, solemn speech praising the teams unspecified actions in a classified operation. Never one for children, Grabowski made a special effort to speak to each son and daughter, gently encouraging each, emphasising that their fathers were all true heroes of whom they could be exceptionally proud.

None of the families were given any indication as to what the men had achieved - or why one had to bury an empty coffin. The only clue they had was all five men were posthumously awarded the Order of the White Eagle, Poland's highest decoration.

The families filed from the room, shaking hands with the assembled dignitaries, accepting their expressions of condolence. As she passed, Grabowski grasped Wojciech's wife's hand in a firm handshake, "I am terribly sorry for your loss. Your husband was an exceptional man."

"Yes," she agreed, "Yes he was."

Grabowski held her hand a little longer, staring hard into her eyes, "Thank you."

Wojciech's wife nodded meekly, gathered her two daughters and left. As she stepped into the corridor she looked at her hand and the folded piece of creased, worn notepaper that Grabowski had left there.

***

Moje kochanie,

If you are reading this, the worst has happened and I will not be coming home. I am so sorry that I will not grow old with you, nor hold you in my arms again. But I thank you for the wonderful years we did enjoy together.

It will take time for the pain to lessen, to come to terms with your loss. But I know you are strong, that you will survive and thrive. And that you will continue to do an amazing job of raising our girls.

Instead of regret, I hope to have left the world a better place. A place that is safe for our girls to grow up, where terror, violence and fanaticism have been banished far from our home.

I will always love you, Urszula and Oksana.

Wojciech x

Before you go...

I sincerely hope you enjoyed reading *The Warsaw Gambit* as much as I did writing it.

If you did, could I please ask a favour - leave me a quick review to say what you did (or did not) like about the story? Your reviews make all the difference to us indie authors - without them, no one finds (or reads) our books. And for some of us, that means we can't eat...

These links will take you direct to the relevant review page:
US: https://www.amazon.com/review/create-review?&asin=B0CR5STG46
UK: https://www.amazon.co.uk/review/create-review?&asin=B0CR5STG46
Australia: https://www.amazon.com.au/review/create-review?&asin=B0CR5STG46
GoodReads: https://www.goodreads.com/book/show/204476273-the-warsaw-gambit

If you really, really enjoyed the story, how about letting a friend know? You could even buy them a copy if you're feeling super generous:

1. Go to the *The Warsaw Gambit* eBook's product

detail page on Amazon.
2. In the **Buy for others** box select the quantity you want to purchase.
3. Select the **Buy for others** button and then enter the details for your gift recipients. If you didn't provide a recipient email address, instructions on how to manage your books are emailed to you after the order is complete.

Thanks again for for taking the time to read *The Warsaw Gambit*.

Until next time…

Benjamin Lloyd

Other books by Benjamin Lloyd:
Misadvertised: A DI Carson Mystery

About the author

As a child at primary school, Benjamin Lloyd was regularly sent on creative writing classes by his teachers. So naturally he went on to study forensic science before falling into a career in IT.

Some years later, he returned to what he does best - words. Working as a freelance copywriter for global IT brands he has written millions of words to help sell computers, software and services. In between ebooks and advertorials, he also writes a successful travel blog, *Journey into Darkness*, with his wife Linda.

The Warsaw Gambit is Benjamin's debut novel, four-and-a-half decades in the making.

He lives in Essex, UK with his enormous family.

Find out more at:
https://www.tech-write.co.uk
https://www.journeyintodarkness.co.uk

Misadvertised: Chapter One

Despite the blaring soundtrack, it had been a quiet night at the Greenwich Real Rock Restaurant, just two tables booked and zero walk-ins. With only four covers and handful of takeaway deliveries to serve, Paolo had sent most of the staff home early.

Now here he was alone at 10pm on a Tuesday night, having to mop the floor of the restaurant himself. He slammed the soggy mop down hard on the floor, watching rivulets of soapy water slosh under the tables and into the shadows beyond. Having to clean the restaurant was bad enough but, but because he was going home early, his wage packet would be down again this month. It was definitely time to find a new job. On the plus side, he would never have to listen to another Adele record at maximum volume ever again. Hopefully.

Lost in his thoughts, Paolo didn't notice the hooded figure emerge from the kitchen behind him. He couldn't hear the tiptoeing footsteps over the sound of Sam Smith earnestly and joylessly warbling out a Donna Summer disco cover on the video screens that surrounded the restaurant. Couldn't react as the figure battered him over the head with a huge battle axe.

Paolo collapsed to the floor, blood spilling from a gash on the back of his head. Stunned, he tried to crawl away, but his hands kept slipping in the claret-coloured puddle that was forming on the floor underneath him.

The polished concrete was slick, no way to get a purchase, no chance of scrambling away from whatever, *whoever*, had hit him. Slipping again, he rolled onto his side, looking up at the hooded figure who stood over him.

"Too bad you're not going to be able to *Lick It Up*," muttered the masked figure, pushing Paolo back down onto the floor, pinning him with his foot. Then he swung the weapon again, grunting with the effort before bringing it crashing down onto Paolo's head for a second time.

Misadvertised: Chapter 2

"Listen Eva, the nights are getting colder and I feel like we've been making progress together. Please can I move back into the house? I'll sleep on the sofa until you're comfortable with having me around?" Detective Inspector James Carson bellowed at his hands free.

"No, not yet," his wife sounded like she was crying, voice rising in tone and volume as she spoke, "I don't care if it was for work or not, You *lied* James. You let me think you were *dead*. You were gone for two whole years and not once did you think to send a text or pop me a postcard or something. Just silence. For *two years*. You couldn't trust me enough to tell me what you were doing and that broke my heart James. I don't know if it will ever heal."

"Look love," he tried to calm himself, to soften the tone of his voice, to slow the pace of the conversation and Eva's spiral into despair, "I'm truly sorry. It was an unavoidable, horrible part of the job. I know it will take time, but I'm doing everything I possibly can to win back your trust. That's never going to happen if I freeze to death in the bloody shed though."

"Come on James, you were gone before I even got out of bed this morning. I can hear you're in the car heading off to a case, which means you're going to be out all hours until it is solved. You won't even be at home long enough to talk, let alone sleep."

Carson winced, "Listen, we'll talk about it when I get home."

"No, we won't," she shouted.

The line clicked, Eva was gone.

"Love you too," Carson yelled at the silence, smacking the steering wheel in frustration, "Argh!"

"Well that was bloody uncomfortable," said DS Leyla Hewson after allowing Carson a moment to regather his composure - and refocus on the road.

"Why?"

"Because most people don't discuss personal disappearances and marriage breakdown in front of their colleagues," Hewson tried to explain, "Especially not the ones they have only been partnered with for a few weeks."

"But why not? Is it a woman thing?" Carson asked.

Bloody hell, he's not even joking, Hewson thought to herself, "I can see why you became a cop."

DI Carson shot his sergeant a puzzled look.

"Anyone would think your brain didn't work like the rest of us," Hewson laughed.

"Most of the time I'm grateful for that," the Carson said, matter-of-fact, "And just for the record, I didn't 'disappear'."

"No judgement from me guv," Hewson held her hands palms up towards him. She had seen just about everything in her line of work already and didn't want to get dragged into a domestic situation, not least because her colleagues were constantly grilling her for dirt on their new boss, "None of my business, not my problem. And quite honestly, I don't want to hear about it either. This is between you and your wife."

"One word of warning though Hewson," Carson said, giving her a steely sideways look, "probably best not to mention any of this to our colleagues. Operational secrets and all that."

Hewson made a cartoon gesture of zipping her mouth shut, all the while wondering how a domestic argument classified as an 'operational secret', even if he was her boss. She turned her attention to the traffic, scanning every car as she always did, looking for a specific silver vehicle.

Carson pulled the car to a halt behind a large white police van and jumped out as though the fraught conversation with Eva had never happened, like a switch had been flicked and he'd leapt straight into 'cop' mode. Hewson scurried to catch up as they strode through a scattering of lightweight steel patio tables and chairs towards a chrome-framed glass door.

"Real Rock Restaurants," Hewson read the neon sign aloud, "Your sort of place, sir?"

"Only the first two-thirds," Carson replied, "Something these places no longer have."

"I never took you for a fan of cheesy chain restaurants, guv."

"Once upon a time these places were super cool, Detective Sergeant," Carson said wistfully, "Rock stars really came here to eat. Sometimes they even played impromptu gigs for their fellow diners."

"Back in the last century I'm guessing?"

"Oh yes, the first one opened in the early 1970s, the very epitome of rock star cool. But I doubt any self-respecting artist would be seen dead here these days. I know I wouldn't. Now it's all about branded t-shirts, crap cocktail glasses and staring at loud pop music videos while munching generic burgers and ignoring your dining companions."

Carson' seemed to be preparing to launch into a rant, but was thankfully interrupted by a fluorescent-jacketed PC, apparently one of the first on the scene. The female officer's face was pale and drawn and she smelled like vomit, a few lumps of recycled breakfast caught in the strands of black hair that had escaped from under her bowler hat. She spoke like she was having a waking nightmare, "WPC Jayawardene sir. We got the call from the day shift manager who arrived to unlock and set up for lunch."

The WPC paused to gesture to a woman sat at one of the outdoor tables, tearful and traumatised, "She found the body and called us immediately. We were super careful not to touch anything sir. And we made sure we all threw up out here in the bushes. But…"

Her voice trailed off as she tried hard not to remember what she had seen. Carson was recording everything in his notebook, a long series of bullet points that would continue to grow until the case was solved. The strangest thing was that although they had only worked together for a few weeks, Hewson had rarely seen Carson refer back to his notes. It was like turning events into written words created an indelible record in his memory.

Carson nodded his thanks to WPC Jayawardene, then continued towards the restaurant. They walked past another uniformed officer dutifully vomiting into one of the potted palm trees that dotted the patio and in through the restaurant door. Hewson tried not to smirk at the young copper's discomfort. Carson didn't even seem to notice.

Inside, it looked like an abattoir. Or what Hewson imagined an abattoir run by Freddy Krueger and Michael Myers would look like. Her stomach lurched, she didn't feel like smirking any more. There was blood splattered on every surface, from fine droplets to significant arterial spray, floor to ceiling. Like someone had used a garden sprinkler to redecorate the restaurant. Puddles of congealing red spread across the polished cement, drawing their eyes to the victim who was splayed in the middle of the floor. He was laid on his back, arms outstretched, posed in total surrender. He was also conspicuously missing his head, helping to explain the source of all the blood.

Leaned up against the table nearest the body was a large battle-axe. On closer examination she realised it was actually a 4-string bass guitar, one side shaped and painted to look like a battle-axe. In amongst the copious amounts of blood smeared on the instrument,

Hewson could just make out the black sharpie smudge of an autograph. Gene Simmons.

"Well, someone had a *crazy, crazy night*," Carson noted drily.

Misadvertised is released on April 27, exclusively on Kindle.

* * *

Printed in Great Britain
by Amazon